The Austen Girls

LUCY WORSLEY

Illustrated by Joe Berger

BLOOMSBURY
CHILDREN'S BOOKS
LONDON OXFORD NEW YORK NEW DELHI SYDNEY

BLOOMSBURY CHILDREN'S BOOKS
Bloomsbury Publishing Plc
50 Bedford Square, London WC1B 3DP, UK

BLOOMSBURY, BLOOMSBURY CHILDREN'S BOOKS and
the Diana logo are trademarks of Bloomsbury Publishing Plc

First published in Great Britain in 2020 by Bloomsbury Publishing Plc

A catalogue record for this book is available from the British Library

ISBN: PB: 978-1-5266-0545-0; eBook: 978-1-4088-8204-7

2 4 6 8 10 9 7 5 3 1

Typeset by Westchester Publishing Services

Printed and bound in Great Britain by CPI Group (UK) Ltd, Croydon CR0 4YY

To find out more about our authors and books visit www.bloomsbury.com
and sign up for our newsletters

This book is dedicated to Katherine Ibbett,
with whom I have danced at many balls

STEVENTON RECTORY HAMPSHIRE

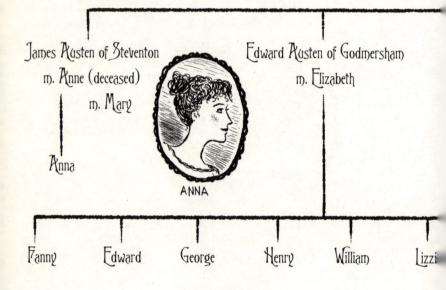

James Austen of Steventon
m. Anne (deceased)
m. Mary

Anna

Edward Austen of Godmersham
m. Elizabeth

ANNA

Fanny   Edward   George   Henry   William   Lizzi

FANNY

the AUSTEN FAMILY TREE

Mr & Mrs Austen of Steventon

Cassandra Austen   Jane Austen

JANE

*Jane also had several
other brothers:
George, Henry,
Francis and Charles

Marianne   Charles   Louie   Cassie   John

GODMERSHAM PARK
KENT

Contents

Chapter 1

Fanny's bedroom, Godmersham Park

'The belle of the ball!'

Anna was looking at herself in the mirror, pulling at her long curly hair, twisting it, piling it up on her head, letting it all fall down again with a theatrical sigh. 'Will I get more partners with my hair up, or down?'

'Oh, Anna,' said Fanny. 'Your hair will fall out if you pull it about so much. And when did you suddenly become Lady Full Of Herself? What if no one asks us to dance at all?'

Fanny herself was on her knees, down on the Turkey carpet, picking up the pins Anna had swept off the dressing table and scattered on the floor while pinning up the hem of her skirt. She sighed. Of course Anna had left it far too late to get the skirt hemmed properly. Fanny's thumb was still sore from the emergency tacking she'd done without her thimble, as a favour for her disorganised cousin.

Fanny's own dancing dress was laid out waiting on the bed, almost as if a proper lady's maid had done it, that extra lady's maid her mother said they needed at Godmersham Park, but which her father insisted they couldn't afford. Gown, stockings, slippers. She'd had everything organised, yet here she was at the last minute, down on the floor in her chemise. It always seemed to be like this, with nine brothers and sisters, not to mention her cousin. Always someone else to look after. Always someone else to put before herself.

But Fanny's predicament, as usual, completely passed Anna by.

'Fanny,' Anna continued, suddenly serious, 'do you have a secret feeling, deep down, that you'll never, ever get a husband?' She was pouting at her own reflection, turning her head this way and that.

Fanny dug her fingers into the soft, rich, comforting carpet. Would she ever find a real-life husband? Would she even find a partner to dance with at tonight's ball? She just didn't know. But what she did know was that getting married was the only topic she, her cousin and her sisters ever talked about here at Godmersham Park. Marriage – a 'good' marriage, as Fanny's mother always said, to 'the right sort of man' – was the goal towards which Fanny's life had been building.

Fanny often imagined that moment of the proposal, the way she would gasp, clasp her hands to her mouth and run, run, ever so fast, to tell her mother and sisters and Anna what had happened.

She couldn't really imagine what would come next, or what it would be like to be married. Or even what the man doing the asking would look like. The proposal, that was enough. That was all she wanted.

In her most private thoughts, though, Fanny worried that all her sisters and cousins, all the other girls in Kent, indeed all the girls in England, would be engaged to be married before she was. Surely she was too quiet, her hair too limp, her skin too flaky, for anyone to choose her.

Fanny imagined herself growing older, her carpet growing threadbare, the mantelpiece empty of invitations to balls … her mother often said how awful it must be to be a spinster.

'Mmm,' Fanny said at last, doubtfully, unwilling to answer her cousin's question. She gathered up the fallen pins by popping them between her lips. That would give her an excuse to keep quiet. Anna had somehow poked her finger into Fanny's fear of not doing the right thing, of disappointing her parents. As she always did. Anna was like that – she generally said what everyone else was thinking but dared not put into words.

Standing up, Fanny started to pluck out the pins, and to prick them neatly back into her pincushion, a raggedy affair that had been a birthday gift from her younger sister Lizzie. Anna now noticed in the looking glass what Fanny was doing.

'Fanny!' she said, throwing up her hands, her hair unravelling again. 'Pins in your mouth! You'll swallow one and choke to death!' She wrapped her hands round her throat, bulged out her eyes and began to mime a person choking to death.

Fanny couldn't help but smile, which of course made some of the pins fall back on to the carpet.

'Frances Austen,' her cousin now declaimed solemnly, as if at a funeral, 'lived for nearly sixteen sweet years on God's earth before choking on a pin. My friends, she was a good girl … yet she died an old maid. No man in the counties of Kent or Hampshire would have her.'

'All right, all right,' Fanny said, laughing, and abandoning the pins at last. 'You're right. Despite what my mother says, I probably won't ever get a husband. I can't think who'd ask me. And I don't know why *you*, all of a sudden, think that you're going to be the belle of the ball.'

'It's a trick,' Anna said. 'Aunt Jane taught me, it's a trick of the mind. You tell yourself, and tell yourself, that a certain thing is going to happen, and you start to believe that it's going to happen, and then … it does. So I've decided that I *am* going to find a husband, and get married, and have a home of my own, because I really, really must. Because I can't bear not to have one any longer, and I'm going to do it tonight!'

'Oh, Anna,' said Fanny. 'Slow down. This is only just the beginning. Nobody finds a husband at her very first ball.'

'Oh, *Fanny*,' Anna replied, almost crossly. 'What a dreamer you are. Lots of girls find their husbands at their very first ball. It's the best chance we've got! You've got to strike while the iron is hot, and people think you're fresh and new.'

She was staring at her own reflection again, and there was something a little grim in her face.

Anna was nervous too, Fanny realised. Despite all her fine words and tricks of the mind.

Fanny patted her cousin's shoulder and turned away

from the dressing table. Although she'd been doing her best to pretend to look forward to the ball, she'd been feeling a little sick all day.

She'd been telling herself that it didn't matter all that much, that it was only one winter evening, a quiet country ball in the quiet county of Kent.

Her debut into high society wasn't life or death. Of course not. It would be silly to think that it was.

'Finding a husband *really is* a matter of life or death, you know, Fan.' Anna was now strangling herself with her bunch of dark hair, brutally tightening it around her neck, lolling her head to one side and rolling her eyes like a corpse.

What a ridiculous girl, Fanny thought fondly. Anna was so … *loud* and funny and confident and beautiful, the whole time. Of course she would find a husband easily.

Whereas Fanny wasn't any of those things. She loved her sisters, she loved reading … she never knew what to say to people. She was boring. Unlike Anna.

It was at that very moment, when Anna was in the final throes of her death agony, that Fanny's mother came in.

It was obvious at once that Elizabeth Austen was in one of her states.

'Girls! What *are* you doing?'

Fanny's mother was looking round the room aghast. Fanny had to concede that it did look as if a whirlwind had come in, rummaged round, and swooshed back out again. Anna always had that effect. She seemed magically to extract every item of clothing Fanny owned out of her presses and cupboards and throw them all down on to the floor.

Elizabeth Austen stood, her hands on her hips, and groaned.

'Girls,' she said seriously. 'You are not ready. You are not even *nearly* ready. It's as if you're not taking it seriously! This first ball of your first season, you know, is a matter of—'

'Life or death!' Anna shouted, twitching in her corpse-like pose half in and half out of her chair.

Fanny was torn between whether to laugh, because Anna *did* look so ridiculous, or whether to try to appease the storm that must surely follow.

To her surprise, Elizabeth's pouchy cheeks quivered as if she was amused as well. In unkind moments, Fanny's brother Edward would mimic their mother's way of nibbling at a bread roll. He made her seem just like an inquisitive, twitchy-nosed guinea pig. And now, instead of exploding into one of her rages, Elizabeth stepped forward and picked up Fanny's gown from the bed.

She held it up to her own ample shoulders, pointed out one toe, and sighed.

'Oh!' she said. 'I remember when I could get into a dress this tiny, and how I used to dance. I danced all night! We all did, my sisters and I.'

For a second, she stood still, lost in her memories, rather than bustling ferociously about as she did most of the time.

Fanny stood up and went over, joining her mother in admiring and stroking the dress.

'Do you like it, Mama?'

Elizabeth had been too busy to see the finished gown when it had arrived from the dressmaker's the previous day. It had been Anna and Lizzie who'd been there by Fanny's side, hooting and whooping, as she undid the box.

'Very nice, dear,' she said. 'But choose a brighter colour next time. White will make you look like a village girl, not a Miss Austen of Godmersham.'

'But, Mother!' Fanny said. 'Aunt Jane said that white was the only colour for ...'

She faltered. In retrospect, Aunt Jane's words seemed a bit too ludicrous to repeat. Fanny also couldn't be sure whether she'd been joking, like she so often was. Fanny looked again, doubtfully, at the white dress, and wondered if it was really … all right.

'Aunt Elizabeth,' said Anna authoritatively, standing up, 'Aunt Jane said that Fanny *must* wear white. It's the colour for a heroine at her first ball, and Aunt Jane said that Miss Fanny Austen of Godmersham Park must *surely* be the heroine of the ball.'

Fanny wished she had just one jot of Anna's confidence. For this had been exactly what her mother wished to hear.

'You're right, Anna,' she said. 'Miss Fanny Austen will be the belle of the ball, and I suppose it's for the best that she should wear white. Modest and demure. Everyone will be looking at you anyway, Fanny! The eldest Miss Austen all grown up! Oh, how you'll glow inside. I remember that feeling of all the gentlemen watching you as you begin the first dance.'

Something else seemed to occur to Fanny's mother. She tossed the dress back on to the bed – carefully, so it wouldn't be creased – and grabbed one hand of each girl, pulling them down beside her on the mattress.

'You might,' she said, more thoughtfully than usual, 'be feeling a little nervous. I do remember that too. And you're such a nervy girl, Fanny. Anna's much more like I was. But remember this. You must show the other young ladies how to behave. You're from Godmersham Park! You have standards to live up to! Everybody in Kent knows that Mr Edward Austen is the most important gentleman in this neighbourhood. Don't forget.'

Fanny tried to peer round her mother's substantial bosom to see what Anna made of that. She knew something of Anna's feelings about the grand Kent-based Austens of Godmersham Park, as opposed to her own less-grand family, the other branch of the Austens who lived in Hampshire.

But now her mother was rattling on, much more in her usual manner. 'I mean to get you two girls off *quickly*,' she said, 'as there are so many of your sisters, Fanny, to get off too, and a quick start sets the pace. Mrs Lewes already has three daughters married! And not one of them yet twenty.'

She prepared to stand up, pitching herself forward to get the momentum to stagger to her feet.

'So it's quite unnecessary,' Elizabeth Austen said briskly, 'to feel at all nervous. The dancing will be over in no time, and you'll be plodding up the aisle, and then children will come, and you'll miss your lost youth, like I do. Now, let's get you dressed.'

At once she began to whisk round the room, her little feet moving with remarkable speed. She was here, there and everywhere, picking up stays, quickly and firmly lacing Fanny into them, giving two twists to Anna's hair that made it look better than anything Anna had yet achieved, and only growing impatient towards the very end, with the clasp of Fanny's seed pearls.

'There!' Elizabeth said, surveying her handiwork. Fanny wished for the umpteenth time that her own fine hair, so colourless, was luxuriant like Anna's. However carefully she tonged it, Fanny's pale hair never held a curl.

It had been a long time since her mother had looked at her, really looked at her, like that. Would she pass muster?

But Elizabeth's guinea-pig cheeks raised themselves up into a slow smile.

'Good luck, girls!' she said, with satisfaction.

Then she dropped her voice, as if she thought that nobody would hear. 'I'm certain they'll be married before Christmas,' she said.

Elizabeth pointed to the door. The general had given her orders. Fanny and Anna nodded at each other and stepped forward. There was no choice. There was no going back now.

Chapter 2

The stairs, Godmersham Park

Just outside the bedroom door Anna stopped so suddenly that Fanny cannoned into her cousin's back.

The obstruction was her father, on the landing in his best coat, the one that made him suck his stomach in before he could button it up. He now stuck out his leg, and eased himself into a low bow.

'Quite charming!' he said. 'You look charming, girls. And your carriage awaits!'

Elizabeth was smiling and clasping her hands.

'Oh, Mr Austen,' she said. 'Look how … *marriageable* the girls are! Very pretty indeed!'

She lowered her voice to continue, but Fanny's

mother's idea of a whisper was just as loud as a normal person talking at a normal volume, and Fanny could hear her perfectly well.

'They'll be off our hands in no time,' she said in his ear. 'Then just four more of those great hungry useless expensive girls to go!'

Fanny could feel her cheeks turning pink. Being bowed to, by her own father, was all so very different from being told off for running, or shouting, or for not watching her little brother and he could have fallen under the horse's hooves and did she not have eyes in her head to see and suchlike.

Her father beamed and resumed his normal height.

'Not really girls any more,' he said in his jovial way, as if he were addressing his fellow landowners at a political dinner. 'The girls have become young ladies. Young ladies!' he repeated, so loudly that the townsfolk of Canterbury several miles away might possibly have been able to hear him. 'But there's still work to be done. We must get them hitched!'

'Mr Austen! What an inelegant expression!'

Elizabeth's tone rose to match her husband's. They often spoke to each other as if they were shouting across the hunting field.

'HITCHED,' Fanny's father said again, huffing and

puffing and straightening his coat. 'And at the very least,' he continued, 'they can dance tonight with that nice Mr Drummer. He's a fine young fellow.'

'Mr Edward Austen!' groaned his wife, striking a blow on his arm. 'No, and no again. Not Mr Drummer. He's beneath the attention of the Austen girls, even Anna.'

Fanny wondered who this Mr Drummer was, not having heard the name before. But it was Anna who forced the question into her parents' torrent of talk.

'Mr Drummer … ?' she managed to say.

'Clergyman! Appointed him to the parish – got it all signed and sealed this afternoon.' Edward had already lost interest in the subject, and was taking Fanny's elbow to escort her down the stairs.

It occurred to Fanny, with a twinge of dread, that her father would be doing exactly the same thing in an hour's time. He'd be leading her into the ballroom beneath the eyes of all the gentlefolk of Canterbury.

Fanny's skin suddenly felt hot, and she remembered all over again that she was nervous. She could almost sense the pressure of people watching and wondering if she would be chosen by a gentleman. It was more than just a dance. As Anna said, it could, it might, lead to a proposal.

But how could she possibly find herself a husband and make her parents happy, if she couldn't even picture what this imaginary man might be like?

Fanny's mother, of course, had more to say. 'We don't just want the girls *married*,' she continued, at volume, 'we want them married *well*!'

At that, there was a ragged cheer from somewhere up above.

'What's all this hullabaloo?'

Fanny and her father turned to look back up the staircase. The balustrade above was crowded with little faces.

It was as if a signal had been given, and a horde of her sisters, and indeed some of her smaller brothers too, all came running down.

'Children!' Elizabeth was exclaiming. 'You were all sent to bed hours ago!'

But there was no stopping them.

In their nightgowns down came Lizzie, Marianne, even tiny Louie, all of them, Fanny could see, thoroughly overexcited. Mrs Sackree, their nurse, was going to have a long evening of it, she thought.

'An-na! Fan-ny!' they were chanting, like little savages. 'Married! Married!'

'Want to see the *dresses*,' wailed little Louie, who had

delicate feelings, and who'd been left behind by the rest of the stampede.

'Oh, show them, show them,' Edward said. 'They'll be on the market themselves soon enough. Better show them what it's like.'

Fanny felt strangely awkward, even though these were only her sisters whom she knew as well as her own fingers and thumbs. She wasn't used to wearing such a naked-feeling dress with its low neck.

'Ooh, lovely,' shouted Marianne, 'lovely dresses, and they'll dance … like this.' She spun round and round, as if locked in a partner's embrace.

Fanny waited for her mother to explode. But then she realised that both her parents were just watching Marianne. They had what Fanny might almost have called foolish smiles on their faces.

'That's what it was like, hey, Elizabeth?' her father said. 'But the season for wine and roses was all too short, wasn't it? All too short.'

And then the moment was over, and Elizabeth was turning away, and scoffing.

'Now, Mr Austen,' she said severely. 'No more talk of clergymen. You've been picking up ideas from that sister of yours. Fanny *should* marry money, and Anna …

must marry money. Clergymen never have any. And please steer the girls well clear of anyone in trade.'

'It's true that my sister introduced Mr Drummer into the parish,' her husband conceded. 'Lord knows where from, exactly, but he's a very brainy fellow.'

'Your sister Jane!' Fanny's mother snorted. 'She doesn't like clergymen enough to marry one and get herself off our hands.'

The little girls had started whooping again, but their mother's voice cut through the din. 'Less of this, if you please!'

'But, Mama,' said Marianne, flopping her bottom down the stairs one by one, 'you said yourself that Fanny and Anna *must* marry –' she bumped down one step more – 'and never mind Fanny's hair or Anna's temper, they must keep a sharp lookout for a husband.'

'Marianne! I'm so ashamed.' Elizabeth spoke sharply. 'What a thing to say.'

'*But you said it!*' Marianne's voice was rising in pitch.

'I may have *said* it,' Elizabeth scolded, 'but it's not to be repeated. And certainly not *in front of the servants*! Now, back up to the nursery.'

'To be fair,' Anna said, 'you did say it, Aunt Elizabeth, we all heard you. Although I think Fanny's hair is very nice.'

A sudden silence.

Fanny squirmed. As ever, Anna had gone too far. If only she'd remember she wasn't really a member of the family, and that she didn't have the right to say pert things like the little girls did.

The stillness was deafeningly loud.

Her mother made it clear that Anna had done wrong by simply failing to respond.

'Mrs Sackree!' Elizabeth was saying instead. 'Come down this instant and take these wicked girls to bed. And now, for Heaven's sake, Mr Austen, get these two to the ball and … well, no need for any further discussion.'

Mr Austen at last succeeded in setting off down the stairs at a stately trot. Once she was on the move, something different from dread, something rather like excitement, finally began to surge into Fanny's stomach.

Oh, we're off at last, she said to herself, *here's the carriage. Our first ball truly has begun.*

Chapter 3

The Star Inn, Canterbury

Fanny bounced at least an inch into the air at each bump in the road. Her father always made their coachman, James, drive slightly too fast.

She sensed rather than saw the passing park as they hurtled through the darkness, towards the town and the Star Inn. She'd have felt the cold of the night, Fanny was sure, if she hadn't been burning up with elation and alarm combined.

Gradually she realised that Anna was discoursing authoritatively about something or other.

'Well, Uncle Edward, if I get the chance, *I* certainly mean to waltz,' she was saying. 'I don't care if the prim-and-proper people round here think it's indecent. They waltz at Almack's in London, I've read it in the paper, and the Duke of Wellington goes there.'

Edward Austen was spluttering and protesting, but Fanny could tell that his heart wasn't in it. He enjoyed hearing his favourite niece insisting she *was* going to try the scandalous new dance.

'Just don't dance with clergymen, either of you,' he said, in the end. 'And if you do, or if you get involved in any of the newfangled waltzing or suchlike, promise me you won't tell Mrs Austen.'

'All right!' said Anna. 'We won't tell. Fanny, you'll waltz too, won't you? Uncle Edward says we can ... as long as we don't tell Aunt Elizabeth.'

Fanny grinned into the darkness. She didn't plan to do any waltzing, but it was nice to be asked.

The sound of the wheels changed as they passed on to the paved road, now swooping down the hill into the town. To Fanny it suddenly felt all too soon to be arriving, her nerves flustered, her hair surely messed up.

But they'd halted, and Anna was shoving the door open, and the deep cold air was rushing in. She jumped down, trying not to get horse manure from the street on her satin shoes.

'I wasn't expecting to encounter *ordure* this evening,' Anna grumbled, grabbing Fanny's shoulder for support.

Anna was wearing a precious new pair of pumps, Fanny knew, a gift from her own parents. Anna's brown dress was just a hand-me-down from another lady living in Hampshire.

Fanny tried to push down the sudden recollection of the cost of her own gown. She knew that Anna had been shocked when she'd heard its price.

A lantern marked the entrance to the Star Inn, and then they were going up the wide staircase, up, up to the dancing room. They could hear the scraping sound of violins tuning up.

But where was the buzz of conversation? The sound of the crowd?

'Early, God damn it!' Edward said. 'After all that, we're early. Never mind, girls, you can make a grand entrance next time.'

Inside the long ballroom, there were so few people they could see all the way through to the blazing fire-place at the other end. It hardly looked like a ballroom at all, just an empty room.

Had Fanny braced herself … for this?

But the Star Inn was famous for its winter balls, to

which came all the gentlefolk of Kent. Fanny had heard so much about them, every winter of her life: what dances had been danced, who'd received a proposal … and now she was really here at last.

Perhaps, with its candles, the room did have something of a glamorous, glowing quality after all. The air smelt rich and sweet.

And it seemed that tonight London fashion had come to dance too. Seated stiffly on a row of chairs were people she didn't recognise. They weren't speaking or moving except for the languid beat of one lady's fan. They were well dressed – *too* well dressed. Fanny could imagine her mother clicking her tongue in annoyance at the sight of someone more fashionable than herself.

Oh, Fanny cringed. How silly she'd been even to half believe Anna when she'd said that Fanny's would be the prettiest dress in the room.

She shrank back behind her father. Her white gown now seemed dowdy compared to the rose-and-yellow outfit of the lady with the fan.

But it was very difficult to disconcert her father.

He went stomping ahead, Anna keeping pace with him, patting her hair, fluffing her brown skirt, turning her head to the side. Fanny knew that she was trying to show off her profile. It really was the most striking angle of her face. Yet Fanny secretly thought it just looked like Anna was turning her nose up.

'Good evening!' Edward was saying. 'I see Sir William isn't here yet, so we will just have to do the honours and introduce ourselves. I am Mr Austen, of Godmersham Park, outside the town, you know, a subscriber to the Star Inn Ball for many years, and this is my niece Miss Austen, and my daughter, who is ... erm ... Miss Austen too. Two young ladies. This is their first ball!'

Fanny died a little inside. Why did he have to mention that? It made her and Anna look so ... unsophisticated.

But there was no time to worry about that now. The moment had come for which they had long been practising in Fanny's bedroom. Fanny glanced at Anna, and knew she was thinking the same thing. They stood side by side, crossed one ankle behind the other, *locked the knees, locked the knees, that was the secret*, and together, slowly, they curtsied. There! It was done. They'd been introduced to strangers, making them officially 'out' in society, and therefore ready to be married.

Fanny stood back up again. It hadn't been that bad. If anything, the room was so astonishingly empty that it was almost an anticlimax.

She'd been concentrating so hard on her curtsy that she hadn't heard a word of the introductions. The rosy lady was extending a gloved hand, returning Fanny's clasp so limply that she feared that the fingers inside might actually be dead. But now, who was this? Fanny felt an unaccustomed thrill running down her spine. Here was a young man with glowing golden hair, and curious dark smouldering eyes, bowing down before her. She noticed, with a little shock, how long his black lashes were, long as a girl's. She herself had that same combination of pale hair and dark eyes, she knew it was odd, but on him it was striking … almost beautiful. He didn't look up through his long lashes, though, as she found herself wishing that he would. Instead, he lazily tossed his longish hair back into place as he stood, and then … sat back silently down on his seat.

Fanny felt disbelief. He'd just sat down again! As if he had no intention of talking to her. Could he really … yes, he was! … he was examining his nails. As if he had all the time in the world.

Fanny could hear her father chatting to the young man's friends, Anna putting in a word here and there, and then here at last was Sir William, the master of ceremonies, a red-faced, squashy-looking gentleman, who often visited them at Godmersham, and who'd known Fanny since she was tiny.

'My lord Smedley!' he was saying to the golden young man. 'Here's the charming Miss Austen. Her very first ball, you know. Won't you invite her to dance?'

Fanny had been teetering between triumph and disaster all evening, but now everything seemed to have come together in a golden explosion of wonder. The ballroom! A dance partner! And now it seemed that she would be opening the ball, her first ball, hand in hand with a member of the aristocracy.

She imagined her mother's proud smile.

She curtsied again, trying to look demure, not smug. For once everything was going just as it should.

She was looking right at Lord Smedley, getting ready to say yes and yet trying not to appear *too* eager, when the blow came.

Lord Smedley looked up, looked away, looked back at his nails.

'I'm afraid,' he said, distantly, tossing out the words as if tossing down banknotes to pay an unwelcome debt, 'that I don't dance.'

Fanny's stomach plunged down, down through the floorboards, down to the stables below. How mortifying!

She opened her mouth, but closed it. She'd almost

said, far too quickly, 'Of course, of course, I do apologise for having ...'

Having what? Having assumed?

It had been Sir William, she reminded herself, who'd suggested they dance.

But Anna was there. And of course, Anna would be on Fanny's side.

'How strange of you, my lord,' she was saying, loudly, as if to draw attention to his strangeness, as if he were the odd one, not Fanny.

She put her arm through Fanny's, making as if to draw her away to somewhere much more exciting.

'How strange it is, Sir William,' Anna continued, at even higher volume, 'that my lord Smedley here says he doesn't dance, yet has come to a ball! He must have been mistaken as to the purpose of the gathering.'

The conversation between the young lord's rosy companion and Fanny's father faltered and died, and they turned to see what was happening.

'I'm afraid,' Anna concluded triumphantly, 'that his lordship has mistaken the Star Inn for the barber's shop, and thinks that very soon the *manicurist* will come along to cut his nails!'

There was a burble of laughter; even the rosy lady

joined in. Fanny herself pretended to laugh as well while she and Anna turned away to go to sit by themselves.

Anna had helped, but it had still been humiliating beyond measure.

Chapter 4

The ballroom, the Star Inn, Canterbury

'Miss Austen? Miss Fanny Austen?'

It was a young man, a real young man. But Fanny was so cowed by the evening's disastrous start that she could scarcely raise her eyes to look at him.

Half an hour later, the Star Inn's assembly room was looking much more like a proper ballroom, and was positively packed with people. But Fanny found herself stranded primly on a chair. She wished she could take her gloves off her sweaty hands. She could sense wisps of hair round her face as if her knot was coming loose.

More importantly, though, she hoped that if she kept completely still, no one would notice her. The first dance had been and gone, and she'd suffered the shame of standing up for it with her own father. Anna, of course, had seized the hand of Sir William, and had ended up opening the ball with the master of ceremonies.

The best that could be said of the first dance was that it was over.

Fanny peeked through her lashes at the person before her. He was bowing, so she could only see the top of a curly brown head. But – oh no – she could also glimpse beetle-black breeches. Fanny realised, with a sinking of the heart, that he must be one of her mother's dreaded clergymen. Not a nobleman. Not even rich. Just a boring church-mouse clergyman.

'May I beg the pleasure of knowing if you are Miss Fanny Austen?'

But wait a minute, Fanny thought, this was much more like a ball was supposed to be. Here was a young man seeking her acquaintance, and doing it in an unortho-dox manner. He hadn't sought an introduction through Sir William, but had come marching straight over as if he could not bear to remain unknown to her one second longer.

Fanny's bruised heart gave a tiny little skip.

She forced herself to stand, curtsy and speak to him. She was beginning to see that in the ballroom everyone must chat to strangers as if they were old friends – as Anna was doing on the other side of the room – or else sink like a stone.

He placed his hand over his heart.

'I am Mr Drummer,' he said, 'and I've recently had the honour of being appointed to the parish of Godmersham. But I haven't yet had the pleasure of making the acquaintance of the daughter of my new patron, Mr Austen.'

He spoke formally, and with a blush, as if it too cost him some effort to be sociable. Fanny warmed to the uneasiness in his manner.

She now saw that Anna had popped up at his shoulder, ogling him from behind.

'I am delighted to meet you,' Fanny said, taking his cue and talking as if following a script for correct ballroom conversation. 'And this is my cousin, another Miss Austen, just like me. Our fathers are brothers.'

Anna was looking Mr Drummer up and down with open curiosity.

'Oh, but we've heard about you!' she said. 'You've just been appointed to the parish of Godmersham, is that right? You'll be living in Fanny's park! Or at least, in the parsonage in her father's park.'

He hung his head a little.

30

'I hope … the tidings that have gone ahead of me do me credit,' he stuttered.

Fanny wasn't sure what to say, for it seemed improper to reveal that her father had called him a brainy fellow, and that her mother had already forbidden her from marrying him.

'Let's sit down,' Anna suggested, 'and we can tell you about some of the people here. We know a few of them, at least, don't we, Fanny? They'll be your parishioners.'

'Thank you,' he said, with pink cheeks, and suddenly all three of them smiled. It was nice to be newcomers together.

With one of the cousins on each side of him, Mr Drummer was soon doing his best to pick out the people Fanny and Anna were able to name among the ball-goers. The tune drew to an end, the two lines of dancers parted, and suddenly they could see right across the room to the moody Lord Smedley, sitting alone on one of the seats opposite.

'And that,' said Anna, 'is the rudest young man that we've ever met. He refused to dance with Fanny! Refused! At her very first ball. Can you believe it?'

Nevertheless, Fanny thought she saw Lord Smedley glancing back at Anna with something like interest.

'I can indeed,' said Mr Drummer. 'That's Lord

Smedley, the viscount, isn't it? I've heard of him. I believe that he's known as The Comet, in London, for his habit of burning up his money.'

Despite having relaxed, Fanny's gut contracted once again. So the man who'd turned her down was not only a lord, but a lord who was rich. She thanked Heaven that her mother wasn't here, because Elizabeth would doubtless have caused a scene or made Fanny try again. She looked round furtively for her father, but Edward Austen was happily occupied in bellowing at some older ladies in the corner.

'Rude!' Anna was saying. 'Abominably rude!'

Mr Drummer was looking at Anna with some amusement.

'Well, you are a young lady with strong opinions,' he said. 'And this is reminding me of something I read recently, a most remarkable novel, called *Pride and Prejudice*, it was, about a young lady's debut in society. It may be that The Comet has hidden qualities. It may be, of course, that he's just shy.'

Fanny brightened at once.

'Oh, I think I've read the very same novel!' she cried. 'It's hilarious, isn't it? And it all turns out so well in the end. You're right, our lord over there does remind me of the prickly hero.'

32

Mr Drummer gave the broadest grin he'd yet achieved, and as he turned to her to enthuse about the book, she noticed that his eyes were brown and warm.

'Mr Drummer, you are too charitable by far!' Anna cut in on the conversation. 'What do you think, Fan? Isn't he too kind?'

Fanny's head told her that Mr Drummer was right to be charitable, but her heart told her Anna was more likely to be correct. 'Well,' she said, 'it may be impolite of me, Mr Drummer, but the gentleman in question seems awfully rude. Quite unlike you.'

Mr Drummer smiled shyly back at Fanny. She began to feel that perhaps her first ball hadn't been an entirely horrible experience after all.

Chapter 5

The breakfast table, Godmersham Park

The breakfast table the next morning was just as noisy and tea-slurpy and toast-crunchy as normal, but Fanny felt even less inclined than usual to join in the Austen family banter and shouting.

She'd come up from such a deep sleep after her late night that the familiar noises seemed to reach her ears belatedly, as if having travelled through deep water.

She sat quietly, crumbling a piece of bread between her fingers. She was wrapped up in her memories of the music, the coloured dresses, the heat.

After Mr Drummer had managed to cheer her up, they'd danced, and danced again, and before long the evening had picked up pace and begun to whizz past in a blur of partners … Anna's smiling face being whisked across her vision … champagne ices to suck upon in a vain attempt to cool down … more dancing … Mr Drummer saying he thought her white gown quite the nicest in the room … how pleased he was to find a partner who loved reading as much as he did himself …

'… and he owns a great estate, and eventually we danced, simply because I grabbed his hand and wouldn't let go until he did, and he was a great waltzer, and … and … and … !'

Fanny realised that Anna was regaling the whole family with her account of how she'd eventually forced a reluctant Lord Smedley to dance with her.

'Drunk,' explained Edward to Elizabeth. 'He gave in and danced with her because he was putting away the old champagne, and he was drunk, and this miss here –' he nodded at Anna – 'went where others feared to tread! Went right up to him and insisted that he was going to dance, and he smiled stupidly, and didn't have the wit to say no!'

'Anna! You are so wicked!'

It was Marianne, all agog, clearly longing to be old enough and bold enough to dance with a nobleman herself.

Anna smiled complacently. 'He's called The Comet,

you know,' she said, 'because he blazes through the ball-rooms in town and sets hearts on fire!'

'Oh! "In town"! Is that how we talk now?' Lizzie was astringent. 'We don't say "up there in London" any more, do we, now that we've danced with a real live lord?'

Anna swatted her younger cousin with her napkin.

'Well,' said a soft, deep voice, 'I counsel you, Anna, against comets. He sounds like an awful young man.'

'Aunt Jane! Aunt Jane! Oh, but how can you say that about a lord!' shouted Marianne.

'Spoilsport,' muttered Anna under her breath.

Aunt Jane had finally put down the newspaper which absorbed her each morning.

'Oh pish, Jane,' said Edward, 'let the girls have some fun. I'm sure he won't marry either of them anyway.'

Fanny winced as she noticed her mother's quick frown. Of course, Elizabeth would dearly love to have a lord in the family.

'Is it fun to dance with a drunken young man?' Aunt Jane was asking Fanny's father drily, looking at him over the tops of her spectacles. 'Is it a good use of one's time and talents? I think Fanny knows what I mean, doesn't she?'

How had her aunt known that she hated the Lord Smedley with all her heart?

Fanny nodded quietly in agreement. Yes, she had been scorched by The Comet's burning tail. Anna might flirt and dice with danger, but Fanny herself had no desire for the sport.

'But a lord!' It was Elizabeth. 'Surely, Jane, you make an exception for the aristocracy? Sounds to me like Anna did very well.'

'Well, doubtless the young man will be coming to call, then,' Aunt Jane said. 'What do you think, Anna, will he be paying your uncle a polite morning call today? To pursue the acquaintance?'

Anna looked at the tablecloth. In her heart, Fanny knew that he would not, and in fact might very well have a sore head this morning and possibly not even remember Anna's name.

The silence which answered her aunt's question told its own story.

'The girls,' said Aunt Jane authoritatively, having got the attention of the whole room, 'are in training. They are in training to become heroines, like the heroines in stories and novels.'

'Oh, Aunt Jane!' Fanny burst out. She couldn't help herself. 'I'm nothing like a heroine. No one will ever write a story about my life. Anna, perhaps, but I'm very ordinary.'

But Aunt Jane just smiled at Fanny, otherwise ignoring her words.

'My nieces can't mess around with silly men, or unsuitable men, or bad men,' Aunt Jane now said. 'They need to hold out for someone extraordinary. If indeed they choose to give themselves in marriage at all.'

At that Elizabeth gave a loud *tut* and threw up her hands. But Aunt Jane was relentless.

'How should a heroine act,' she continued, 'as she comes of age, like Fanny and Anna, and makes her entry into the world? No, be quiet, Marianne, let's hear it from Fanny and Anna themselves.'

Aunt Jane didn't often speak, but when she did the family generally listened. Even Edward, curious, shushed some of the children, and stopped crunching his toast.

Anna spoke first.

'We should *be bold*,' she said. 'We must take our destiny into our own hands.'

There was silence. Everyone wanted to hear what judgement Aunt Jane would pass, but instead she silently swivelled her head to look at Fanny.

Fanny's thoughts whirred as fast as one of her brothers' spinning tops. Was there a right answer? What did she … really think?

'I imagine …' she began.

'Well?'

Her aunt was waiting.

'I imagine that we should be *wise*, in choosing who to dance with and so on.'

Aunt Jane smiled. 'Be *both* bold *and* wise, girls. I knew that you two would know what to do and how to behave. I knew it. You have more power than you think. Spend it well.'

Fanny and Anna exchanged glances. It was rare to win the praise of Aunt Jane, but when it came it was always worth having.

But Lizzie groaned, and pushed back her chair in disgust.

'You make it sound like a horse race, Aunt Jane,' she complained, 'with fences to jump. You make it sound like it's really difficult to pick a husband. Surely girls should just take the first one who comes along? Then they can crow about being married.'

'It *is* hard,' Aunt Jane said quietly. But she'd retreated back behind her paper. She'd lost interest in the conversation.

'Oh, what nonsense,' said Fanny's mother sharply, more sharply than she was accustomed to speak, even when the children did evil things. 'A girl needs a husband. Ideally a lord, it's true, but any gentleman of good birth and good fortune will do perfectly well.'

Aunt Jane's intense silence might have signalled her disagreement.

The smaller girls, having received no attention for several minutes, again began to complain and spill their milk and generally act up.

'Don't fill their heads with such nonsense, Jane,' Elizabeth said, in between dishing out admonitions to her offspring. 'Fanny and Anna will marry very quickly, I'm sure, and will be off our hands before any of the other girls from Kent can catch up with them.'

'Of course we will,' said Anna stoutly.

But inside herself, Fanny did not feel so sure. It hadn't been all that easy so far. And here was a new question popping into her mind. Why, for example, hadn't Aunt Jane, who was so clever, got married herself? Had she somehow failed in boldness and wisdom? Hadn't anybody wanted her? Or maybe the husbands on offer hadn't been extraordinary enough for Fanny's aunt?

One day, Fanny thought, *I must ask her.*

Chapter 6

Hurstbourne House

Aunt Jane disappeared off to her room after breakfast, to do whatever she did in there by herself, but Fanny couldn't stop thinking over her aunt's advice. It had been almost as if Aunt Jane wanted her and Anna to delay, to think carefully. Whereas everyone else seemed to want them married quick-sharp.

Aunt Jane does talk balderdash, Fanny said to herself, shaking her head. These were words she'd heard her mother say ever so often. She was bustling along towards the housekeeper's room, a big pile of bed linen in her arms. *Mama must surely be right*, Fanny mused. *If I don't marry as soon as I can, I'll be hanging around, and I'll spoil the chances of Lizzie and Marianne when they come out in society. That wouldn't be fair.*

But what if the first man who asked her was awful? What then?

The sheets in Fanny's arms had been shoved into the linen press any old how, and had come out with great jagged creases. She hoped that her mother would raise her eyebrows, and nod, and congratulate Fanny for having detected the mistake.

'Quite the little housekeeper – I can rely on her' was one of the things that her mother sometimes said about sensible Fanny, but never about her sisters.

But today in the housekeeper's room the feeling was frosty.

'Creased, are they?' Fanny's mother said over her shoulder. 'Well, put them back in again, straight this time, Fanny, there's a good girl.'

Fanny turned to leave, but Elizabeth's hand had mysteriously appeared on her wrist.

'Thank you for noticing,' her mother said unexpectedly. 'I know you always do it properly. And dance well tonight, Fanny! Don't let Anna steal all your partners.'

Fanny went off back upstairs with a lighter step, even if the linen was growing heavy in her hands. Her mother had reminded her that whatever may have happened yesterday, tonight was a fresh beginning. There was another ball to come! Another chance!

As darkness fell, she and Anna were once again squished into the carriage, and then Fanny's father was ushering them up the steps into Hurstbourne House. It was the home of their neighbours, the Hursts, who always hosted the second ball of the season.

Anna and her father were swept off into the drawing room, where the guests were gathering, but Fanny thought she might steady her nerves by taking a private peek into the room where the dancing was to be. Like a soldier assessing the field where a battle was to be fought.

The big dining room looked unusually empty because its table and carpet had been cleared away, and its chairs pushed back around the edge. And all at once, with a skip of her heart, Fanny saw Mr Drummer. He was talking to the musicians, trying to sing them a tune to see if they knew it. He had a clear, high voice, Fanny thought to herself, watching him throw back his shoulders and laugh at something the violinist said.

And then, as he turned his head towards her, she saw his face light up as he spotted her approaching nervously across the polished floor.

'You look like a skater,' he said, bowing and taking her hand, 'sliding along like that!'

'This floor is so slippery,' she said. 'It will be perfect for dancing.'

He smiled, and raised his arms as if to welcome her into them.

The violinist, seeing what Mr Drummer had in mind, struck up the elusive tune, or something like it. Fanny took to the floor with him in a delicious little private waltz of their own. She discovered that a huge ridiculous smile was plastered on her face.

A couple of hours later, though, Fanny was having much less fun. She was sitting on a chair in the corner of the same room, now so crammed full of the Hursts' noisy friends that it was terribly hot, even though the tall windows were open to the black sky outside.

She'd danced with Christopher Hurst, and again with Mr Drummer, but it hadn't been as magical as when they'd danced almost alone to the violin.

Fanny sighed, looking round for Anna. Anna too had danced with Mr Drummer before slipping out of Fanny's sight. Although Fanny couldn't see Anna, she now thought she could hear her cousin's whoop. Her eyes followed Anna's voice, and she saw that her cousin was in the arms – indeed, in the close embrace – of … was that? … Yes, it was! The haughty Lord Smedley. It certainly looked like him. It *was* him!

Fanny gave a nervous little gasp. Lord Smedley was looking down at Anna through his long eyelashes and the floppy golden fringe which grew across them. He'd even unbent enough to allow a half-smile to pass across his sullen face.

Fanny half rose to her feet, but sank back at once. The sight of Anna with such pink cheeks, laughing too loudly and clinging to the lord, made her stiff and tense. It was correct to have fun at balls, to show that you were willing, her mother had explained that. But Fanny had a prickling feeling *this much fun* was not something of which Elizabeth Austen would approve.

Her instinct was confirmed. Before Fanny could do anything else, she realised an older lady seated on the chair next to her was also staring at Anna.

And the lady was tapping the arm of her other-side neighbour and saying something. She was holding her fan before her mouth, but Fanny was close enough to hear the words.

'Cavorting,' her neighbour was saying under her

breath. 'Of course, he'll never take a penniless girl like her. And I don't think any of the other young men in Kent will take her either after this performance.'

Fanny sat up straight, pretending that she hadn't heard a thing, cheeks ablaze. She had a plummeting sensation in her stomach on Anna's behalf, and had to blink her eyes very hard.

It's just the heat, she told herself. Her eyes were only watering because she was hot and tired. She got to her feet, to find her father, and to say that they must get Anna and go home.

The evening, which had started so beautifully, had been spoilt. Only two days in, and the husband hunt was already going very badly indeed.

Chapter 7

The dairy, Steventon Rectory

Fanny could see that Anna was frustrated enough almost to kick the pail right over. She kept giving it vicious little taps with her foot. It rocked, the milk in it sloshing from side to side.

'It's going to tip,' Fanny warned.

Anna gave an exasperated growl.

'Hampshire is soooo boring!' she said.

Of course, it could be that spilling the milk might release some of the anger that Anna had been bottling up inside herself ever since they had left Godmersham and come here to Anna's home at Steventon.

Fanny returned her attention to her cloth and to getting on with cleaning the tiled dairy counter. She'd clearly have to do all the jobs herself. Since Anna had danced, twice, with Lord Smedley, she'd been far too full of herself for anything like work.

Anna now nudged the bucket even harder, and a tide of milk frothed over its edge.

'*You'll* have to clear up that mess,' Fanny warned her. 'I'm not doing it.' She was pushing her luck, she knew, by saying anything critical of Anna. Her cousin was just impossible when she got into a state like this.

Sighing again, more loudly than ever, Anna heaved up the pail and lugged it to the bench where the skimming dishes lay waiting for the milk. She got the big scoop. Moodily and badly, she began to fill the dishes.

Fanny, for her part, was enjoying the work in the dairy, even if most of it was just mopping up after Anna. If Fanny and her sisters ever went to the dairy at Godmersham Park it was just for fun. At Godmersham, the cream was destined for after-dinner ice cream, not just for boring old everyday butter. But it was butter that they were in the process of making here at Steventon, and Anna's stepmother expected them to do it every single day.

The door opened, and in came Anna's stepmother, Mary. Fanny called her 'Aunt Mary', for although she wasn't a real aunt, she'd been married to Fanny's uncle

James since Anna had been tiny. Aunt Mary came stamping in, bringing with her the smell of the rain outside. Her broom was in her hands as usual. She was 'capable', was Aunt Mary. People always called her 'that capable woman, James's wife'.

'Oh, Anna,' she said. 'Isn't it finished? Daisy used to take half the time!'

Daisy was the dairymaid who'd recently disappeared from the rectory. Anna had told Fanny her private belief that Daisy had run off because she could no longer tolerate even one more day of Aunt Mary's supervision.

'Well, *Daisy* knew what she was doing!' Anna cried. 'She was a proper dairymaid! That was her job!'

'And now it's *your* job,' said Anna's stepmother. 'You need to learn to run a house and farm. You'll have to support your husband's business, you know!'

Anna looked as if she wasn't listening. For a second, Fanny saw her as Aunt Mary must see her: ungracious and ungrateful.

When Fanny's own mother taught her things around the house, she was always eager to learn, eager to get a bit of her mother's undivided attention. She would never think of answering back. But then, Fanny realised, she learned because she wanted to learn. Aunt Mary seemed to think that Anna *had* to learn, as if she had no choice.

Perhaps that was right. Fanny knew that Anna wouldn't get a dowry from her uncle James. Aunt Mary was only trying to prepare Anna for marriage to a farmer, or someone else who needed to earn a living.

By contrast, Fanny's mother thought that earning money was somehow a dirty thing to do. Much cleaner and nicer to inherit it. And that, clearly, was what Anna thought too.

'I'm not going to have that sort of husband,' Anna was explaining. 'I'm going to have a rich one, who can employ a dozen dairymaids, so that I need know *nothing about it*!'

Fanny winced. She knew Anna was thinking of Lord Smedley. But she also knew that when Anna had danced with him, for that surprising second time at Hurstbourne House, it was only because Anna, like the lord himself, had drunk too much French wine.

Aunt Mary's broom wasn't wielded with a great deal of force, but it was definitely with a smack that it came down on Anna's behind.

'Anna!' her stepmother almost shrieked. 'You're always like this when you come home from Kent. You're so ... *dissatisfied* with your family and your home. I'm sorry, Fanny,' she added quickly, seeing Fanny's hurt face, 'but it's true. Your mother and father give Anna ideas above her station.'

Anna clenched her fists. Fanny could tell she'd very nearly raised her hands and simply swept the china dishes on to the floor.

When Anna tried to speak, her voice was all wobbly. It was embarrassing and awful. Fanny stared hard at the milk, wishing that she could simply disappear into its still, white peacefulness.

'It might be good enough for you, living here, like this,' Anna was saying to her stepmother, her words coming out very small and strangled. 'But I ... want ... more.'

With that, Anna whipped around to face Aunt Mary. Perhaps she wanted to see what effect her words might have.

Aunt Mary's scarred face, pocked from long-ago smallpox, fell into a picture of dismay.

And Fanny saw that after a second, Anna's expression softened too. It was as if hurting her stepmother hadn't given her the pleasure for which she'd hoped.

'I know you long for a better father and mother,' Aunt Mary said quietly, turning the broom in her hands. 'I know that you would like to be a Miss Austen of Godmersham, not of Steventon. But truly, your father tries so hard for you, Anna.'

Aunt Mary and Fanny waited awhile, aware that Anna's anger was somehow spilling away into silence.

'I've invited Mr Terry to tea,' Aunt Mary said hopefully, as if offering a much younger girl a treat. 'Mr Austen has been asking me to have him over. I don't think he's very exciting, but he's said to be a nice young curate. You girls can practise your conversation on him.'

'A clergyman!' scoffed Anna. 'Fanny's mother says that clergymen are to be avoided like the plague.'

'Erm, except Uncle James, of course,' Fanny added quickly, feeling that Anna was a little tactless to pass her mother's views straight on to a clergyman's wife.

And she and Anna now exchanged half-smiles. For of course Anna's saying the word 'clergyman' had reminded them both of Mr Drummer ... of 'Dominic', as Fanny had discovered that his Christian name was, by sneaking a look at the parish register.

She and Anna had spent a good deal of time discussing Mr Drummer's views on this and that, and following his recommendations for novels. They'd gone walking with him, listened to him in church and poured his tea on several occasions.

But of course, they didn't think of him as a potential husband. Fanny especially knew her parents would never approve of that match for her. She could just picture her mother's face! But it did make her wonder if Mr Terry would be rather nice too.

'Come on,' said Aunt Mary, wearily, 'let's call a truce. You can leave the butter for now – I'll do it later. But, Anna, I want you to be pleasant to Mr Terry.'

They all went out into the muddy yard.

'How long is it until you go back to Godmersham?' Anna asked, falling back and asking Fanny quietly. 'Maybe I can come and visit you again?'

Fanny knew what she was thinking about. Escape.

But it was as if Aunt Mary ahead of them had read Anna's mind.

'Real life's not like that silly story, you know,' she called back to them. 'What's it called, *Pride and Prejudice*? Where the heroine ends up with the big house and that gentleman you girls keep talking about.'

By now practically everybody Fanny knew had devoured the most deliciously romantic story she'd ever read.

'Well, you don't know that for sure,' Anna said, addressing the mud rather than her stepmother.

'Daffodils?' asked Aunt Mary hopefully, changing the subject. Fanny realised that Anna's stepmother was trying to divert her. Everyone knew that Anna loved picking and arranging flowers.

'All right,' Anna said, with bad grace, and trudged off towards the garden to find some for the tea table.

Aunt Mary and Fanny looked after her, watching her dark hair getting wet and bedraggled in the warmish rain, her skirt splashed with mud.

'Poor Anna!' Aunt Mary said softly. 'She wants to live in a different world.'

It was true. The set of Anna's back as she went signalled that she rejected everything in the rectory, in the village of Steventon, and even in the whole muddy county of Hampshire.

But no matter how much Anna wanted it, Fanny thought, her dissatisfaction wouldn't make Lord Smedley come to rescue her.

Chapter 8

The drawing room, Steventon Rectory

Two hours later, Fanny was amazed by the way her cousin had somehow turned herself into a very different person. Anna had scrubbed her face at the pump in the back yard, smacked at her hair with a brush, and changed into her prettiest muslin dress, the one with all the buttons.

Fanny had much less to do, for she'd managed in her neat way to get much less wet and dirty than Anna.

And now Anna was in a better mood. Even a tiny tea party, with just one young man and two young ladies, was better than nothing. She seemed determined to enjoy it as much as she could.

'What would Aunt Elizabeth do?' Anna wondered out loud to Fanny, opening the shutters and scanning the dusty drawing room. Fanny tried to think of ways to make the old, low room more like the comfortable magnificence of Godmersham Park. Her mother, Fanny thought, might complain a lot, but she did work very hard at making the place pleasant for her family and all their guests. Her own home, Fanny now realised, was a warm house, warm with her mother's love.

'We could perhaps light a candle,' she said.

'It's useless,' Anna said. 'This place will never look elegant.' But she went to light a candle anyway, even though twilight was still some hours away. She was in the very act of striking the flint when Aunt Mary came in.

'Anna! We don't need that,' she said at once. There's plenty of light for Mr Terry to see.'

'But it would make the room cosier!' Anna said, annoyed.

'And it would cost us a shilling.'

There was no answering that. Anna grimaced at Fanny. Fanny knew that her cousin felt constantly trumped, blocked, disappointed by the endless question of pounds, shillings and pence.

'But you *can* light the fire,' Aunt Mary conceded. 'Your father will want to dry his trousers. And when

Mr Terry arrives, I don't want you berating him about the evils of the slave trade. Try to be demure.'

Anna pulled the expression of a mule. 'Aunt Jane,' she said drily, '*loves* berating people on the evils of the slave trade. And no one stops her.'

Making a fire was a different and much less attractive proposition than lighting a candle. It involved putting on aprons and going outside again and lugging wood.

But after they'd made the effort, the room did look more welcoming. On the tea table lay the pot, the cups, and a plateful of sliced seed cake that Aunt Mary had made.

'I hope she won't claim it as her own,' Anna whispered to Fanny.

Anna's stepmother felt there was nothing shameful in baking cakes herself.

To Fanny's surprise, there was a movement in the corner. Anna's father must have come into the room unobserved, and had been sitting silently in his high-backed chair. Perhaps snoozing, Fanny suspected. His spectacles were halfway down his nose.

'Pretty buttons,' he said to his daughter.

'Thank you!' Anna said lightly.

Fanny sighed. Any compliment, even if it was just from her own father, left her red and trembling. But

Anna took praise almost as her due. She was lifting her nose into the air now, and Fanny guessed what she was doing. Showing off her profile again.

'Anna!' hissed Fanny. 'You look ridiculous like that.'

A little sheepishly, Anna snapped her chin back down, as if for reasons unknown she'd just been examining the ceiling.

There were sounds in the passage, and Fanny could hear talk of the rain, and the roads, and the Hampshire mud. Aunt Mary was bringing in the visitor, who was rubbing his hands and looking bedraggled.

Anna put her nose in the air again. It seemed that she just couldn't help it.

'Terry!' said her father, straightening his angular legs with the usual noisy complaint from his joints.

James Austen was shaking hands with the newcomer. Fanny now saw, with a sinking of the heart, that he was not at all the 'young' man Aunt Mary had promised. Mr Terry looked almost as old as Anna's father. He was wiping the rain from his spectacles before putting them fussily back on to his nose.

But he was a man, and she and Anna were young ladies. They had better get on with being charming; that was what they were supposed to do.

Anna's father and Mr Terry began to talk, of Latin authors Fanny had not read, and of clerical grudges, and vengeful deans of whom Fanny had never heard and hoped never to meet.

He seemed a poor stick, this Mr Terry, agreeing with Uncle James on everything. Anna cleared her throat, then offered him some tea.

'Oh, no, let me pour myself for the young ladies.'

He'd made the offer a little too late, but at least he'd noticed them, and seemed conscientiously determined to be polite.

Mr Terry brought a teacup to Fanny, and then took another to Anna, who was sitting winsomely on a stool by the fire. As he drew near the flames, Fanny noticed that despite his stoop and his awkward manner, his face was a little less lined than she expected, and his hair was cropped short rather than completely bald.

'Do you enjoy literature yourself, Miss Austen?' he asked her.

'Oh, my daughter and her cousin like to wallow in trashy novels,' said Uncle James dismissively. 'They have no time for the greats.'

'I am not as literary as my father,' Anna said, meekly, for Mr James Austen's poems were known – and the reading of them was dreaded – in the neighbourhood. 'But I do like a good book. Perhaps not as much as my cousin Fanny, who is the greatest bookworm I know.'

'Of course,' said Mr Terry. 'I like a love story myself.'

Fanny tried to disguise her surprise. Really! He didn't look as if he did.

'This new book about, oh, the moody dashing gentleman and the spritely Lizzie, I enjoyed that most thoroughly.'

Anna smiled. 'Oh, you mean *Pride and Prejudice*? That's a brilliant book. Fanny made me read it, and I think even my father might enjoy it. The misunderstandings! The happy ending!'

He was smiling back at Anna now. Fanny noticed that her cousin's face was all aglow. She'd once again become the Anna Fanny knew, the one full of jokes, who was called 'a caution' by all the servants at Godmersham Park.

To Fanny's surprise, Anna stood up.

'I'm going to show Mr Terry the pleasure grounds,' she said, in a manner that brooked no argument. 'It's not raining so very much now, and I want to get his opinion on the shrubs.'

Fanny was clearly not included in the invitation. *So, I'm to stay behind and make conversation with my aunt and uncle*, she thought a little resentfully.

Anna did not immediately leave the hearthrug, though, as if waiting for the inevitable comment that it was too wet, too late, too wasteful of time to traipse about in a shrubbery. Fanny knew that Anna had slightly oversold the shrubbery's attractions by referring to it as a pleasure ground.

And yet, Fanny thought defiantly, feeling sorry for her cousin, you could hear the nightingale on a summer evening at the far end up near the woods.

'Oh yes,' she said. 'Mr Terry *must* see the pleasure grounds.'

Anna held out her hand, and, as if irresistibly drawn by the force of her gesture, Mr Terry took it. And he indicated, clumsily, but in an extremely genteel manner, that she should precede him out of the door.

Chapter 9

Anna's attic bedroom, Steventon Rectory

'You were an awfully long time out in the garden with Mr Terry,' Fanny said, between strokes of the hairbrush.

Anna was already tucked up in the bed she was sharing with Fanny in her little room up in the eaves of Steventon Rectory. But now she bounced out of it once again. It was as if she could not keep still, even for a minute.

'Oh, Anna, be careful with the feathers,' Fanny sighed. Anna had started prancing about while trying on Fanny's own new Sunday bonnet. Fanny wished she'd packed it away in her box rather than leaving it out on Anna's dressing table. Or rather, on Anna's plank of wood balanced between two chairs.

'Mr Terry!' Anna snorted, in something like disgust. 'Do you think that Lord Smedley would like this hat?'

She gazed at herself, apparently enraptured by her own reflection as it hovered by Fanny's shoulder in the looking glass. Propped up on the plank, the mirror leaned precariously against the faded blue wallpaper.

'I think,' said Fanny, 'that he'd probably describe it as a bonnet for a bumpkin. My mother doesn't really approve of it. Not London-y enough.'

'Hmm.' Anna kept her own counsel, and Fanny could tell that she didn't really approve of it either. 'Did Aunt Jane help you choose it?'

Fanny smiled.

'Oh, Anna,' she said. 'You know that my mother won't let Aunt Jane take me shopping. No, I chose it myself.'

She gave a few more brushes, but only really for the show of it. It was always quick to comb out her fine hair, whereas Anna usually took ten minutes and a lot of wailing to get through hers. Fanny realised that she was overbrushing her hair because she was nervous about what she was going to say next.

'Anna,' she began tentatively.

There was something in Fanny's voice which made her cousin stop preening. Her stance was wary and stiff.

'Yes?'

'Um, you know you mentioned Lord Smedley?'

'What about him?'

Anna's tone was aggressive. She jutted out her chin and pulled the bonnet low across her eyes.

Fanny groped for words, but found them not.

It really was too difficult to go deeper into these dangerous waters. But Fanny had underestimated Anna's obsession with her dancing partner.

'I think his sister is probably going to write to me soon, don't you?' Anna said, stroking the bonnet. 'He knows I'm here in Hampshire.' Anna had what might have been described as a tremulous smile playing across her lips. Her cousin did seem to enjoy playacting these different parts, Fanny thought, the vain girl, the disgruntled girl, the girl who might be in love … 'I'm pretty sure she will,' Anna said complacently. 'Lord Smedley said he would get her to ask me to stay with them, last time we danced.'

Anna and Lord Smedley had danced, Fanny knew, a grand total of three times. If his sister did really write with an invitation for Anna to visit, then perhaps yes, Anna could expect a proposal to follow.

And yet, it had been two weeks since the last ball in Kent, and no letter had come.

'Are you really, truly sure, Anna?' Fanny said gently,

avoiding her cousin's eyes. 'That you're going to hear from him? It's not just that mind trick of Aunt Jane's?'

Although Fanny didn't dare look at Anna, she could tell by a kind of quivering in the air that Anna had grown tense and still and grim again.

She said nothing.

Oh dear, Fanny thought desperately.

'Maybe you're right,' Anna said. To Fanny's surprise, her voice was quiet and resigned. 'An actual lord, let alone a rich one, would be too good for a girl like me.'

Fanny's comb hovered in mid-air. What did Anna mean? Was she serious? Was she being ironic?

Anna now sighed, and hurled herself backwards on to her bed.

'I know what you think, Fanny,' she said wearily, as if casting off her act, 'that Lord Smedley won't really ask me to marry him.'

Fanny still sat frozen before the mirror, worried that this was some kind of a trap. Was Anna trying to get her to say that Lord Smedley was too high a prize for a girl who lived in a shabby old rectory? Or was Anna fishing for reassurance that Lord Smedley really *did* like her after all?

She sat there, thinking, her mouth opening and closing silently. All of a sudden the words came tumbling out.

'It's not his money, or his title, Anna,' she said.

Now Fanny had finally started to speak from her heart, her way was clear. She burned with love for her unhappy cousin. 'I just think he doesn't have a good character.'

But Fanny hadn't quite got the measure of Anna's bitterness.

'All because he wouldn't ask *you* to dance,' she now said scornfully. 'It's easy to mock him and do him down. I happen to *like* his company.'

'Oh, but Anna,' Fanny said, at last giving up fiddling with the things on the dressing table and turning squarely to face her cousin. 'I truly don't think he's kind, or generous. I don't think he'd treat you as you deserve to be treated. I would rather you married almost anyone else but him.'

'What, even a clergyman?' said Anna. Her face was now turned away, but Fanny could see that Anna's hands were plucking brutally at the blanket which covered the bed.

'Why yes, even a clergyman. Or especially a clergyman. They are … you know …' Fanny tailed off miserably.

'Yes, clergymen,' said Anna bitterly. 'They're the sort of men who are supposed to marry a girl like me.'

She said no more, but lay there looking at the wall.

Silence fell.

No nightingales tonight, Fanny thought, hearing the stillness of the woods outside. There really were so few people living in this part of Hampshire. So few potential husbands.

She sighed and blew out the candle, then slipped into bed beside Anna. The silence grew longer and longer, as Fanny couldn't think what to say next. Anna, and Lord Smedley, and the disappointing Mr Terry from that afternoon's tea party all seemed to whir round inside her head, like the dancers at a ball.

When would the music stop? Who would be facing whom when it did?

Chapter 10

The breakfast table, Godmersham Park

Fanny sighed loudly as she wiped Louie's howling face. She was back at home in Kent, while Anna had remained behind in Hampshire. Everything seemed particularly miserable and ordinary at Godmersham, and now Fanny's sister had somehow managed to smear herself all over with porridge.

Their father, though, was happily slurping up a glass of Madeira at the same time as devouring his ham. The noise around the table was almost intolerable, but he barely noticed.

Fanny saw, rather than heard, the door opening, and the footman entering with the post. She saw her mother had spotted this too, straightening up and brightening.

This was the day that the fashion magazines arrived, and Fanny looked forward to reading them with Aunt Jane. It was something they always did quietly together. They generally had to wait for a couple of days, though, while Elizabeth carried them around with her, loudly complaining that she had no time to read them.

But to Fanny's surprise, the footman kept coming, round the table, still holding something, and holding it out to her. A letter!

Well, this was a nice surprise, on yet another dreary day of face-wiping. No one ever wrote to Fanny, except her aunts and uncles on her birthday.

And now she recognised Anna's bold hand. It was extremely rare to get a letter from Anna, because postage was expensive and Anna's pocket money did not go far. Fanny really wanted to save her letter till later when she'd be by herself. But her father had a curious knack of noticing things when she didn't want him to.

'What scrape has young Anna got herself into this time?'

Fanny thought fast. Sometimes Anna wrote things in her letters which weren't fit for the family breakfast table. Sometimes she said things that were particularly unfit for her aunt Elizabeth and uncle Edward's ears, complaints about the blissful, wasteful life at

Godmersham. Fanny occasionally wished that her and her cousin's roles were reversed. Anna seemed so sure that to be a Miss Austen of Godmersham was better than a Miss Austen of Steventon. Anna didn't realise that a Miss Austen of Godmersham was expected to do boring and pointless things too.

She must equivocate.

'You know how bad her handwriting is, Papa!' she said. 'It will take me ages to puzzle it out.'

He was pouring coffee now, and telling Marianne that she couldn't have any, she was too young, and ... after that Fanny lost track of her family because Anna's letter had leaped up and grabbed her by the throat.

Dearest Fanny! Dear, dear, dearest Fanny! it began.

This was a bit over the top, even for Anna.

I am the happiest girl alive. And the unhappiest. Fanny, I know you think I didn't listen, but I have taken your advice. Today Mr Michael Terry asked me to be his wife, and I accepted. But my parents – I really and truly HATE them, by the way – have refused their consent. I simply don't accept this. I consider myself engaged to him, and we love each other most sincerely. Fanny! He kissed me! It was very strange and glorious. I want to tell you all about it.

Now wish me luck, dear Fanny, because I have a bat-
tle ahead – making THEM agree.

It was Marianne who noticed that Fanny was sitting rigid, her eyes still on the paper.

'Well, Fanny?' she said. 'What's going on at Steventon? Is Anna engaged? Has she beaten you?'

Fanny slowly raised her eyes from the paper.

'Well … yes,' she said.

'What nonsense, Fanny,' said their mother. 'Don't make jokes about such a serious business. I wish you girls would take it more to heart – it's not a game.'

'Yes,' said Fanny, louder and more firmly. 'Yes, it's true. That was a lucky guess, Marianne. Anna *is* … engaged!'

Very little made Fanny's father and mother simultaneously put down their occupations and turn to her with their full attention.

'No!' said Edward.

'Yes?' asked Elizabeth limply.

Fanny saw at once that her mother was disappointed that Fanny herself wasn't the first Miss Austen to have accepted a proposal. Fanny had been excited on Anna's behalf, although a bit confused and worried by what Anna meant about her 'advice'. But now she realised that there was another emotion swilling around inside her as well. Was it jealousy? Anna had won the race. Anna had won the prize of being the first Miss Austen to be engaged.

Yes, Mr Terry was only a clergyman, but at least he was a husband. Oh, why had Fanny wasted so much time at the balls she'd attended, by dancing again and again with Mr Drummer? She had to try harder!

She met Aunt Jane's gaze across the table, and winced. It was so unfortunate that Aunt Jane should be looking at her at such a moment. She knew that her aunt would read the shameful, hurt reaction on her face.

'No,' Edward said more loudly. 'That's nonsense. Who is the man? My brother James doesn't know any eligible bachelors, buried away in the countryside. The only place Anna could meet a man worth marrying is here at Godmersham. And you've only just come back from Hampshire, Fanny, and she wasn't engaged then! There's been no time.'

'Fanny,' Aunt Jane now asked seriously. 'Do Anna's parents approve of this match?'

It was, of course, a difficult question to answer. How much of Anna's private business should she give away? Fanny saw that Marianne, for one, was all agog. But Marianne wasn't really old enough for such things.

'Well, no,' Fanny said reluctantly, before deciding that there was no choice but to reveal all. 'Anna says that they do *not* approve. He really has no money at all, and Aunt Mary wants Anna to marry someone with at least a bit. I imagine they are all in uproar at the rectory.'

It was all too easy to picture the scene. Doors being slammed, Anna throwing herself on to her bed in fits of tears and saying that her stepmother, Mary, wasn't her real mother, and didn't really love her.

'Oh dear,' said Aunt Jane. 'I suspect, Elizabeth, that the man in question must be one of your dreaded clergymen.'

'He is,' Fanny said. 'I've met him, of course, he came to tea. He was all right, I mean, there wasn't anything particularly wrong with him. But I wasn't expecting ...'

'I don't dislike *all* clergymen,' cut in Elizabeth. 'What a thing to say, Jane! There are some very good livings to be had in the church, and I wouldn't object to a dean or a bishop for Anna. Then she could live in a palace! But so many of them, unfortunately, are so miserably poor.'

Now there was the violent scraping of a chair being pushed back, right off the edge of the carpet and on to the boards of the floor.

Fanny had rarely seen her father so deeply moved.

Abandoning his plate, he was stalking back and forth, his hands behind his back.

'I must write at once to James,' he said, 'and tell him that this, that this … cannot be allowed to stand. Oh, what is the dratted thing called? You know, a miss … a missa …'

'A *mésalliance*,' said Aunt Jane, quietly. 'But really, you must consider poor Anna. She must be dreadfully upset if she has got herself into a situation like this. What if she's in love? It can happen, you know. Even with clergymen.'

'Love?' said Marianne doubtfully. The word 'love' was never mentioned in any of the Godmersham discussions about marriage.

'Well, at least that Mr Drummer is safely out of the way,' said Elizabeth smartly. 'He was far too young and single and penniless for my liking.'

Marianne had been following the conversation intently.

'What's happened to Mr Drummer?' she now asked. 'We only heard him preach about three times, and then he disappeared.'

Fanny sensed the grown-ups exchanging glances, and knew at once that something had happened while she was in Hampshire. Something they didn't want to talk about. But the grown-ups had also neglected to prepare what to say about it to the children.

She drew herself up in silent resentment. Sometimes the grown-ups considered her as one of them, sometimes they didn't.

But Fanny said nothing, because she wanted Marianne to think that like the rest of the adults, she *did* know what had happened to Mr Drummer.

'Mr Drummer,' said Aunt Jane delicately, when it became clear that no one else was going to speak, 'has been the subject of a most unfortunate accusation. He has been accused of stealing. But we need to know all the facts before we decide what we think.'

Fanny frowned. Really? 'Her' Mr Drummer, as she privately thought of him? Dominic? Surely he wasn't a thief. There must be some mistake.

'Oh fiddlesticks, Jane,' said Elizabeth, with some fire. She too rose up from her chair.

Fanny observed how her aunt Jane went on quietly eating her toast. She didn't appear to be at all frightened. *That's the way*, Fanny thought, *to deal with wrath*.

'He was far too young, too dreamy, no connections, nothing to recommend him at all! It's good riddance. Of course he did it. He wanted some decent clothes! Mr Austen!'

Appealed to in an argument, Edward always tried to make peace. 'Well, well, my dears, let's see, shall we? We really did know very little about the fellow, Jane, and I'm not even sure where you got him from when you rustled him up out of nowhere.'

'I like Mr Drummer,' said Jane, unfolding her paper. 'He's not a ninny, unlike so many of the ballroom creepers with whom poor Fanny has to go out dancing. And I shall do him the honour of treating him as if, like all citizens of this country, he is to be considered innocent until proven guilty before the law.'

'But what about Anna?' cried Fanny, feeling that the adults were getting diverted from the more pressing business. Mr Drummer wasn't relevant to the vital subject of marriage and husbands. Of course not. 'Shall I write at once to Anna and tell her to come here?'

'No, you shall not,' said Elizabeth. 'Oh, do be quiet for once, Marianne!'

Marianne had started to agree with Fanny. Of course, they wanted to see their cousin Anna at this great crisis of her life.

'No, no, she shall not come here,' Elizabeth insisted. 'Let Mr Drummer remain where he belongs, which is well away from this house, and let Uncle James do what he hardly ever manages to do, mainly because he can't get a word in edgeways, and tell her for once that she ... CAN'T!'

With that Elizabeth swept up her magazines, undid Louie's little hands from her skirt and flounced out of the door, pausing oddly before she closed it.

Despite the drama, Fanny half laughed.

She realised that her mother had been on the point of slamming the door – until, that is, she'd realised that that's exactly what Anna would have done herself.

Elizabeth closed it ever so, ever so quietly instead.

Chapter 11

Aunt Jane's bedroom, Godmersham Park

After breakfast, Fanny wandered along the corridor, hardly knowing where to go. The window at the end revealed that the wind was chasing patches of watery sunlight across the grass in the park outside. The seasons were changing, summer was coming. Anna engaged! Anna married! Fanny's mind kept slipping from one thing to another. Her best friend was moving on and leaving her behind.

She could hear, from her sisters' distant shrieks, that they were upstairs in the nursery. Lice had been discovered in the hair of their brother George, and the girls were enjoying watching Mrs Sackree combing them out.

Eventually Fanny remembered what she was supposed to be doing, which was listening to the little girls reading. She marched up to the nursery, extracted her pupils and took them back to the library. Soon, the familiar halting drone from *Moral Tales for Young People* started up, and Fanny's mind wandered off again. Where would Anna and Mr Terry live, if her father did allow her to marry?

She wracked her brains to remember what Mr Terry had actually been like. There was little to go on. She remembered his stoop, his black clothes, and his long silences.

There seemed nothing good about him at all, except for the fact that he was a full-grown, single man with all his faculties. Was that why Anna had accepted him? Was it worth it, just to get a husband?

'Fan!'

Marianne had almost shouted her name. Fanny detached her eyes from the chestnut tree beginning to bud outside the window, and forced them back indoors. She looked at the books, the fire, the daffodils in their vase upon the table, almost with wonder. Nothing had changed, and yet everything had changed. Anna was engaged to be married.

'Oh, that's enough for now,' she said, vaguely. Lizzie

clapped her hands in delight, and the two girls went running back upstairs.

'Are the lice out? Can we see them? How big are they?'

She heard the yells fading as they galloped upwards.

Fanny sighed. What was she supposed to do? Write to congratulate Anna? Anna had promised that she'd be married by Christmas, and it looked like she was going to be as good as her word.

As Fanny prowled through the hall, the mansion all around her was living its many lives, ticking, turning, throbbing with its business. She could hear her mother in the housekeeper's room as usual, planning the day's menu in a torrent of castigation and complaint. No point in asking her.

In the silver room, the maids were hard at work on the forks and spoons. Fanny knew that every one of them would be terrifically excited by the thought of Anna's engagement and utterly in favour of a quick wedding.

She wondered where her father was; probably out on farm business. She half-smiled at the memory of his almost comic anger as he tried to remember the word 'mésalliance' …

Aunt Jane. Of course, Aunt Jane.

Fanny climbed the stairs, running, until she

remembered that she was now a grown-up young lady with a cousin who was already engaged.

But in the passage she speeded up once more. There was the small rug which provided such a satisfying skid if you leaped on to it. She only became demure once more when she reached her aunt's door.

She tapped.

Silence within.

She tapped again, a little louder.

'Yes, Fanny?'

Aunt Jane really was uncanny in her ability to deduce what was going on out of her sight.

Fanny stepped inside. Although there was a view of the luxuriant chestnut leaves outside, the room was small, much smaller than the other bedrooms. But Fanny had heard her aunt saying that she preferred it that way. As usual, Aunt Jane wasn't looking out at the bright green beyond her window. Her long angular figure was bent over her desk.

'How did you know it was me?' Fanny asked.

Aunt Jane finally threw down her pen and rubbed at her back.

'Oh, your mother would have banged at the door. Your father would have marched straight in. The younger girls would have run off after knocking just once, they are far too impatient to wait for an answer, and as for the boys, well, the boys never come here because I have *frightened them away*.'

Fanny knew that if her younger brothers teased their aunt too much and annoyed her, Aunt Jane would pretend to be a witch who could put a spell on them that would make their breeches mysteriously fall down in public.

Aunt Jane, still rubbing her back but more slowly, was looking closely at Fanny.

'Come here, Fanny,' she was saying. 'Come and sit down here. What is it? Is it Anna?'

All of a sudden, at the unexpected sympathy, Fanny found her eyes full of hot and shameful tears.

'I'm not going to put a spell on *you*,' her aunt said, confidentially. 'You are quite my favourite niece. Apart from Anna, of course. Let's talk about Anna. It's confusing, isn't it?'

'Aunt Jane,' said Fanny, giving up trying to hide her swimming eyes and getting out her handkerchief. 'I do love Anna.'

'I know you do,' said her aunt. 'I can see when you two are together that you're just like my own sister and I.'

Aunt Cassandra, as all the Godmersham children knew, was a softer touch than Aunt Jane, good for gifts of sugar candy and shillings. Sparing with punishments, she was always ready to indulge in a game of dressing up or shuttlecocks when she came to visit. Fanny sometimes felt that she alone of all the children appreciated the person of great kindness who lay behind Aunt Jane's more forbidding manner.

'Well, do you think she's right to ... to ... jump at this man? Just because she's desperate? That must be what's happened, don't you think? If she really *liked* anyone, it would be Lord Smedley. But that, um, was never going to work.'

'I really don't know,' her aunt said simply. That was the thing about Aunt Jane; she never lied to you, not even to make you feel better.

Fanny scrunched up her handkerchief in her hand. In some ways, she felt worse than ever. If even Aunt Jane didn't know what she should be feeling, then things were in a sorry state indeed.

'It all depends, doesn't it?' said her aunt, seeing Fanny's distress. 'We need to know more. Does she love him? Does he love her? Is he kind? I fear that he must be poor – because if he was rich I think my brother James would have consented to the engagement at once. My brother's finances mean he'd find it hard to turn down a rich match for Anna, unless the man was known to be cruel.'

'Aunt Jane, I know I ought to congratulate her ... but I can't, I can't. I'm just not sure about it.'

'Fanny,' her aunt said seriously. She beckoned Fanny closer to the table where she sat. Aunt Jane pushed her spectacles down the bridge of her nose, and craned her long neck forward so that she could look over the tops of the lenses and right into Fanny's eyes.

'Poor Anna is under so much pressure to get married,' she said. 'They never leave her alone, do they? We must get Anna here to Godmersham and talk to her properly and find out what's going on. At once.'

Aunt Jane now stood up and began to stalk about.

'Your mother wasn't thinking clearly this morning, she was distressed, but I'm sure she'll agree.'

There was a pause.

'Fanny? Yes? You'd like to see your cousin, wouldn't you?'

'Yes, yes, I would, Aunt Jane. But you know she was here only at Easter, and the stagecoach is very expensive, and if Uncle James is angry with Anna I don't think he'd pay the fare for her to come again so soon.'

'You're right,' her aunt said. 'I've thought of that. I'll offer to pay myself. I really must see my niece.'

Fanny felt able to make the ghost of a smile.

'That's very kind of you, Aunt Jane,' she said.

She paused.

She'd have liked to ask a question. She knew that Aunt Jane didn't have any money, which was why she was living here at Godmersham rather than in a house of her own, and therefore she didn't know how Aunt Jane could afford Anna's coach fare. But she didn't quite know how to put her question into words.

But there was also something else she wanted to ask as well. And maybe she *could* bear to ask it, here in the warm quiet sunlit room with all Aunt Jane's attention focused on her.

'Aunt Jane, why didn't my mother want to invite Anna? She loves Anna.'

Aunt Jane sighed.

'Your mother,' she said, 'is a busy woman. Busy! She has all you children to look after ...'

But Mrs Sackree does that, Fanny thought rebelliously.

'... and your father to please, and the house to run, and the servants to manage, and, oh, you know, so many different people to please ...' She trailed off.

'Aunt Jane, can you tell me why Mama is always so cross?'

Aunt Jane was staring out of the window now, and Fanny knew that she often said important things when she wasn't looking at you. So Fanny listened extra hard.

'Your poor mother,' Aunt Jane said, 'is going to have another baby. That's why she's cross sometimes, and particularly at this moment, and that's why she failed a little in generosity to Anna this morning, although she is, as you know, at heart a very kind and generous woman.'

Fanny gasped.

'Yes,' Aunt Jane said. Her voice was carefully neutral, as if she wasn't either happy or sad. 'Then you'll have ten brothers and sisters, isn't that right?'

'Eleven of us!' Fanny was astonished. Really, another baby in the nursery? Another baby to play with. Another person to look after. Another mouth to feed. 'Well, the little girls will be delighted.'

They did enjoy playing with each new baby as if it were a doll, dressing it up, carrying it about.

But Aunt Jane had said 'your *poor* mother'. Fanny now pictured her mother sinking on to the sofa and saying that she would thank the Lord for a cup of tea and an early night. But however busy or cross she might be, Fanny's mother was always, always there for a kiss last thing at night, and for a spoonful of syrup if you didn't feel well. How surprising to think of her as an actual human being, with a life of her own.

And then, Fanny thought a little grimly, *if the new baby is a girl, that'll be yet another one of us who must find a husband.* Would there be enough husbands to go round?

'Yes,' said Aunt Jane again, vaguely. 'And now, I must, I must finish, um, you know ...' She gestured at her desk.

'Your letter? Yes, of course. And then you'll write to Anna? For us both?'

'I'll write at once,' said her aunt. 'Don't you worry. I'm very good at that.'

Fanny stood and got ready to leave. Aunt Jane was already bent back over her desk.

'Let your mother tell you in her own good time about your new brother or sister! No need to mention that, you know.' She threw the words over her shoulder.

'Yes, Aunt Jane,' Fanny said.

She waited a moment in case her aunt had anything more to say, but there was only the scratching of her pen. Fanny turned and walked out, with a slightly straighter spine.

It had been a thoroughly adult conversation.

And at no point had Aunt Jane pressed Fanny on what was becoming the last thing she wanted to think about: how in the world she was going to find a husband of her own.

Chapter 12

The Hursden Ball

That night, all too soon it seemed, it was time to go out on the husband hunt again.

Fanny put on her pale pink slippers, and her new pale pink dress. She thought it was a good dress for spring, and when she walked into the ballroom at Hursden she found that the whole colour scheme was pale pink too.

'Tulips!' whispered Elizabeth loudly in Fanny's ear. 'The cheap option. You can see they've just got them from the garden outside, as if they might not even have hothouses here. Mr Austen, have they a hothouse here at Hursden?'

But Fanny's father was already heading for the

card-playing in the other room. His disappearing back made her feel bereft. She hadn't yet been to a ball with her mother, and she was worried that Elizabeth would be a sterner chaperone and judge of her performance on the social scene than her father.

Just then Christopher Hurst came up, bowed and asked Fanny for the first dance.

Her heart almost thudded with relief.

Yes, Elizabeth was smiling with satisfaction, and, oh yes, now she was taking herself over to a sofa near the wall, there to rest her feet and talk to her friends, leaving Fanny in relative peace.

'Thank you, Christopher,' she said as they took their places in the set, side by side. 'You've made my mama very happy by asking me to dance right in front of her like that. And me too,' she added quickly. 'I'm glad to dance with you myself! But she wants so much for me to have lots of partners.'

'That's all right,' he said. 'You're a good dancer. You don't stamp on my feet.'

Fanny's smile grew even broader. It was perhaps true that her neat little feet carried her more easily across the ballroom than some of the other partners Christopher probably had to haul around.

'You dance very well, too, Christopher,' she said,

although it was a lie. She remembered, as the players struck up, what an effort it always was to force him to keep time to the music. 'And have you been out shooting today?'

She glimpsed Aunt Jane, crossing the ballroom to bring Fanny's mother a glass of lemonade.

'Getting the hang of this, I see, Miss Fanny,' said Aunt Jane's wry smile.

But all too soon the first dance in the chaste embrace of Christopher from next door was over, and Fanny felt herself to be down on the deck again. Would anyone ask her for the second dance? Triumph or disaster?

George Broadstairs, Steven Armes, Richard Goodall.

One by one, they all saved Fanny's honour.

But with each of them, once the initial glow of relief at being rescued faded, she found herself making the same small talk. Even falling back on the same question about shooting.

Aunt Jane had called the young men of hereabouts 'ballroom creepers', and Fanny could see why. They all seemed so young, and they crept so cautiously around the floor, without much energy or desire.

Fanny longed to be violently twirled into the music of the waltz, one-two-three, one-two-three, turn, and turn, just as Mr Drummer had done the night they'd danced together alone.

Mr Dominic Drummer!

She found herself scanning the faces of the late-arriving guests, but then remembered that he wouldn't be there.

Of course not; he had mysteriously disappeared. And how could she possibly find a replacement who could dance as well?

She sighed so loudly that Richard Goodall heard.

'Miss Austen! Are you tired?' he was saying anxiously. 'Come, let me take you to sit down with your mother.'

It would have been ungracious of Fanny to refuse.

So she suffered the indignity of being escorted right across the crowded floor and placed beside her mother on the sofa.

'Fanny!' Elizabeth hissed. 'I *saw* you sighing and yawning at that poor young man. This simply isn't good enough. Not good enough at all!'

Fanny looked at the floor and shuffled her slippers.

'Sorry, Mama,' she said.

Now she'd have to sit on the sofa looking interested and hopeful, as if she wanted someone else to ask her to dance. And her mother would closely observe to make sure that she didn't go off into a daydream.

The ball had turned into an ordeal, to be got through as best she could without further humiliation. Perhaps all balls would be like this without – well, to be honest – without her favourite dancing partner, Mr Dominic Drummer.

Chapter 13

Out in the park

A few days later, Fanny was lying on her back, looking at the sky. It held traces of cloud, like chalk dust gathered in the folds of a blue cloth, but the cloth itself was a bright, summery blue. And there by her side on the rug lay her cousin. Anna was back at Godmersham.

As soon as Fanny had set eyes on Anna, her heart had melted and her conflicting feelings about Anna's engagement eased. She could see how important it was to Anna that she might soon be married with a home of her own, and would no longer have to be the very least important Miss Austen, poor relation of the many Misses Austen of

Godmersham Park. And how distressed she was at the thought that this husband might escape her.

The problem of Anna's parents' refusal to allow the engagement to stand was burning as brightly as ever. Would Anna get her heart's desire? The tension, not knowing, was both exciting and terrible. Fanny rolled over on to her side to see what Anna was doing.

Her eye fell at once on something that lay between them: an empty bottle.

'Good Lord, Anna,' Fanny said crossly, her mind taken quite away from thoughts of the future, 'have you really drunk all the lemonade?'

Anna sniggered.

'You sound just like my stepmother,' she said. 'Don't *enjoy yourself*, Anna, don't *indulge*.'

Fanny sighed.

'It's not that,' she pointed out. 'I might have wanted some myself.'

Anna was instantly contrite.

'Sorry, Fan,' she said. 'I do know that I can be selfish. But I'm not as selfish as people are always telling me that I am,' she muttered, turning away and ripping up a handful of grass.

Fanny fell back again and looked up at the sky.

'I think that's a cuckoo, isn't it?' Anna asked idly.

'Our cuckoos at Steventon are quite pretty.' It seemed that Anna could afford, at last, to be gracious about the place, now she finally had the prospect of leaving it for good.

'I wonder if Uncle James's letter is well on its way?' Fanny asked. 'It might almost be at Canterbury already!'

She simply hadn't been able to resist returning to the great topic of the day.

'Well, Uncle Edward wrote to him, oh, five days ago now,' Anna mused, 'so that would certainly give a letter time to get there, and one to come back?'

When the Kentish Austens had taken Anna, shaken and weepy, back into their bosom, her pitiful condition had convinced the whole family that Anna's engagement must be allowed to stand.

Anna had wept with rage and frustrated desire in Fanny's room, while Aunt Jane and Fanny herself had stroked her hair. Even Anna's aunt Elizabeth had come rushing in to give her a kiss.

'Never mind, Anna,' she'd said. 'I'll speak to Mr Austen. I'll tell him to tell your father that your looks are being injured by this silly business of his withholding consent.'

'It's not so much my father,' Anna moaned, 'as that bloody Mary.'

Even in Anna's distress, Aunt Jane could not let this stand.

'Bad language is no way to speak of your stepmother,' she said sternly. 'She may not be all soft and cuddly, but she's a sensible woman.'

'And it may be,' said Elizabeth, 'that Mr Austen can do something for the young man.'

'He's not that young,' Anna had sniffed. She'd come around to the idea of having a husband much older than herself, even if thirty (Mr Terry's age) sounded awfully ancient. Anna had decided to think that it made him seem distinguished. If he didn't have a fortune, at least he had the status of being properly grown up.

So more letters had been written to Uncle James and Aunt Mary, imploring them to let the engagement stand, and to ask the 'young man' to come on a visit to Kent as well so that everything could be sorted out.

Fanny's whole body tensed up with excitement every time she thought about the prospect of the letter from Steventon arriving. Would the letter come? Would Uncle James relent?

'What do you think,' Fanny now asked, sitting up, 'my mother meant, when she said that my father might be able to "do something" for Mr Terry?'

'Why, Fanny!' said Anna. 'You goose. Give him money,

96

of course. He hasn't a bean. I wonder if your father has in mind to give him the living of the parish, now that Mr Drummer is gone. Then we could live here, in your parsonage. Mr Terry could replace Mr Drummer easily, I'm sure.'

Fanny was taken aback by Anna's callousness.

'Anna, we were *friends* with Mr Drummer, don't you remember?' Fanny declared hotly. 'He was kind to us, when no one else was. And he loves books – how lucky to have a parson in this very park who likes novels. We can't just replace him. It's all a misunderstanding, I'm sure. He wouldn't steal anything.'

It was, Fanny now realised, as if she'd been trying not to think of him, except as a good dancer, and to forget what had been said. There had been that mysterious conversation at the breakfast table. Her parents had told her not to think about him, and she hadn't. Unlike Anna, she often obeyed them like that.

In retrospect that did seem … odd of her. As if she hadn't a mind of her own.

Fanny suddenly realised that she cared very much about whether Mr Drummer would come back or not, and she could not possibly countenance even Anna living in Mr Drummer's house. But she chose not to put that thought into words.

'I never even asked what had happened to Mr Drummer,' she muttered, to the grass as much as to Anna. 'And Aunt Jane told me to be bold!'

'But your father must have said *something?*'

Fanny could see that Anna was almost incredulous at her lack of curiosity.

'Well,' Fanny said, 'apparently, Mr Drummer was accused of stealing, from a shop in Canterbury. All very embarrassing. And I believe that he might be in the …' She stopped.

Fanny was starting to feel ashamed that she didn't know. 'I think he might be awaiting trial in the House of Correction.'

'But surely Uncle Edward could get him out?'

To Anna, of course, everything seemed easy.

Fanny stared at her.

'Oh, Fanny, you moonstruck calf,' Anna said, holding out a hand to help Fanny up. 'Do you do everything your parents tell you without ever asking why?'

'You're right,' said Fanny. 'I just … went along with what Papa said, which was that I wasn't to worry.'

But Anna wasn't listening.

'Come on then,' she said. 'You'll never become a heroine if you let people boss you around like this. I do like the thought of having Mr Drummer's house, but even

I don't like the thought of his being in the House of Correction. For a crime which he may not even have committed! Stealing! It sounds so unlikely!'

Fanny groaned, but she allowed herself to be pulled to her feet. She hated to bother her parents and draw attention to herself. But she could see that Anna was right. Simple friendship, let alone any other kinds of feelings, compelled her to find out exactly what had happened.

Chapter 14

The library, Godmersham Park

Fanny and Anna went storming down the hill. Fanny's feet were fuelled by a growing sense of righteous indignation about Mr Drummer. She must challenge her father at once to tell her the truth.

She would not be put off by his bluster, his loud laugh, or his general air of blinking bonhomie.

They surged in through the front door, surprising old Pemberton the butler, who was dozing in his tall-backed chair. It was pleasantly cool in the marble entrance hall after the sun outside.

'Where is Mr Austen?' Anna demanded.

He blinked at her sleepily. 'Mr George?' he asked. 'Or Mr Henry? Gone out, perhaps to the woods …'

It was true that Anna was much more likely to be asking for her young cousins rather than her uncle, maybe to organise a game of cricket.

But Fanny couldn't be bothered to explain. She was too indignant. 'Oh, don't worry,' she said, gathering her skirts again. 'We'll try the library.'

Yet when they reached the great polished mahogany door it was dauntingly closed. It looked a little like the lid of a coffin. Fanny's courage failed her. She stood back to let Anna knock.

But Anna had her hands behind her back. She was wearing her mulish expression. Yes, she was definitely going to make Fanny do this all by herself.

Fanny sighed, and tapped.

Inside, the library's tall windows were open, and the white curtains were billowing inward in the breeze. They looked calming and clean. But Fanny's father was looking far from fresh. He was in his shirtsleeves at his desk. He was frowning at a pile of papers, and seemed to be punishing some of them by balling them up and throwing them on the floor.

'Oh, Fan,' he said when he looked up, as if disappointed. 'I thought you were Bond with the market figures.' He turned back to a column of numbers. He started muttering again, adding them up under his breath.

He looked busy, but then he always did. If not now, then when? When else would she get his attention?

Fanny coughed, and stepped boldly forward so that she was looking down on him. She wondered what Anna would do in the same situation, and put her hands on her hips.

Just for a second, though. It took her that long to remember that it was an unladylike thing to do, and she lowered them back down again.

Her father didn't look up.

Ha, Fanny thought. She put her fists back on her hips and kept them there.

'Papa!'

That got him. He laid down his pen and looked up at her, pushing the papers aside, perhaps with something like relief.

'Yes, Fanny,' he said, 'what can I do for you?'

'I would like to speak to you,' said Fanny.

She tried to be clear, like when Aunt Jane captured the attention of the whole breakfast table. She perched herself on the edge of the desk. 'About Mr Drummer.'

Her father's face fell, and he leaned back uncomfortably in his chair.

'Bless me,' he said. 'What about him? That was an unfortunate business.'

'What happened to him?' Fanny cried. 'He was kind, you know, to Anna and me, at our first ball. He talked to us and danced with us when no one else would.'

'By Jove, did he now!' Edward said. 'Yes, he was an excellent young man.'

Fanny sighed. He was missing the point.

'But *what happened* to Mr Drummer? I hear he has been taken to prison!'

'Yes, yes, he has,' her father conceded, turning back to his papers with a shake of the head. 'Stealing. In Canterbury. A bad, bad business. I had no idea that his means were so slender that he felt the need to steal … items of clothing. Gloves, I believe it was.'

'Papa!' Fanny's surprise made her voice a little shrill, and she swallowed hard in order to lower it. 'Really?' she began again. 'I mean, it sounds so unlikely.'

'Well, Mr Fortescue told me,' her father said. 'And he's another magistrate, you know. Fine fellow. Couldn't have got it wrong.'

'And what did Mr Drummer say?'

'Oh, well, I don't know, I've been too busy to see him.'

If he wasn't such a jolly, hearty man, Fanny would have said that her father looked a little mortified. And now he was continuing with his explanation, almost as if he felt a need to justify his behaviour.

'Open and shut case, Fortescue said. No question. Drummer did it, for sure, pop him in the prison to make sure he doesn't run.'

'But, Papa, surely, oughtn't you go to ask Mr Drummer if he really *did* do it? You didn't even visit and ask him? You can't have appointed him to the parish unless you thought that he was, well, a gentleman, and worthy of your protection!'

'Ah, but Fanny, that's the thing. I'm not sure that he was … quite … a gentleman. He was so inexperienced, and nobody seemed to know anything about him. Except your aunt Jane, of course. Ask her about him. Wait, though, on second thoughts, Fanny, *don't* talk to anyone about him, anyone at all. You've your reputation to think about.'

He nodded at Fanny gravely, as if that were the end of the matter.

Fanny felt her heart beating faster. She actually placed her palms on his desk and leaned over it towards him.

'Papa,' she said sternly. 'This young man was in your employment, he was *your* parson, and he has been arrested in a manner that sounds most dubious, and you haven't even taken the trouble to investigate the circumstances?'

'Fanny!'

It was difficult to get Edward Austen into one of his rages, but Fanny realised – too late – that she'd done it. He was on his feet now, towering over her, menacing her from his full height. She slipped off the desk and retreated slightly across the carpet.

'I have ... farmers not paying me, Fanny,' he fumed. 'I have criminals to prosecute all day and all night, it seems! I have ten children, and another on the way, and a ... and a *quite useless and penniless brother* whose daughter won't behave ... and I have mouths to feed, and bills to pay, and worries enough to turn me grey, and I will ... not ... be lectured to ... by a young lady!'

He paused, but only to fill his lungs for another bellow.

'Particularly not by a young lady who *must not*, who *must not*, as your mother keeps telling us, *chase after clergymen*. It would kill your mother, Fanny, and although she rushes about and shouts a lot, you know that she loves you, and wants the best for you.'

He calmed down a bit. 'As do I, my dear,' he added more mildly. 'Your cousin Anna has got herself into a state over that young man of hers. But I know that you are too sensible to take an unfortunate interest in an unfortunate fellow like that Drummer. Find yourself a *proper* man to marry.'

Fanny found that she was shaking a tiny bit, as if a gale had come gusting through the library.

'I just wanted you to …' she began. No, it was no good.

She lowered her eyes to the carpet. Oh, but it was a beautiful carpet, rose and gold and green. A man who owned such a carpet, she felt, could afford to be kind and generous. Something inside Fanny compelled her to go on after all.

'I don't want to marry him,' she said, without raising her eyes, 'I simply want to see justice done. Just … justice.'

'Dear God!' cried her father, coming out from behind his desk, taking her by the shoulder and propelling her towards the door. 'And what do you think justice is, Fanny? The Good Lord gives everyone their destiny. Some deserve it, others don't. Now spare me from the demands of young ladies who think they know best. Just get yourself married, please, dear Fanny. That's what you want too, isn't it? Get yourself married, take yourself off my hands.'

Somehow, Fanny found herself outside in the passage, the door closing firmly behind her.

Inside the room, she could hear the faint sound of her father giving a kind of irritated roar.

She found herself checking her limbs, one by one. Yes, she was intact. No injuries.

Anna was still there, watching her, round-eyed. Fanny suspected she'd had her ear pressed to the mahogany, and hoped she hadn't been able to hear exactly what her uncle had said about her.

'Well?' Anna insisted.

'Um, no good,' Fanny said. 'He wouldn't tell me anything really, or do any investigating.'

But something else was bothering her too, something that wasn't Mr Drummer.

It had been the sentence her father had thrown out almost incidentally. 'We want the best for you,' her father had said. 'Get yourself married, that's what you want too, isn't it?'

A new and mutinous thought was forming itself inside Fanny's head.

She imagined what would have happened if she'd said, right back at him: 'You *never asked me what I wanted*. What if I *do* want to marry a clergyman? Or what if I *don't* want to get married at all?'

But now she crossed her arms, and began to pace up and down the passage.

'We can't let this rest, Anna,' she said. 'We need to know the truth. I'm going to investigate the case. Like a professional thief-taker, you know. We're going to solve the mystery. I think Aunt Jane will probably help.'

If her father would not explain what had happened to Mr Drummer, then she must make it her mission to find out for herself.

Chapter 15

The breakfast table, Godmersham Park

Now Anna was back at Godmersham, the noise level at breakfast-time had risen even higher.

The next morning, only Fanny's father was quiet. He was still in a huff from Fanny's questions, she thought, protecting himself behind a barricade of newspaper like Aunt Jane did.

The little girls, obsessed with Anna now that she was engaged – or at least, likely to be engaged just as soon as that vital letter arrived from Steventon – pestered her with questions.

'Anna, will you let us come to stay at Mr Terry's parsonage?'

'Anna, will you go to his church every Sunday, or will

you stay at home to make your cook roast the dinner properly?'

'Silly bean, she won't have a cook, he's as poor as a church mouse.'

'Hush, Marianne, you ought to be ashamed of yourself!'

Anna smiled and tried to give bright answers. But Fanny could tell that her mind wasn't on the little girls.

It must be clinging like a limpet on to the prospect of a letter from Steventon, the letter that would determine the fate of her life.

'And now,' Anna said, with an air of a person who wanted to change the subject, 'what are we going to do today?'

'I wish I could go to the shops,' said Elizabeth. 'Mrs Sackree has a list of things the children need. Linen, muslin, riding gloves to replace those ones William lost, Lord knows what else.'

'Well, go, then,' said Edward, in his huffy voice. 'I don't need the carriage, and the horses are getting fat and lazy.'

'Oh, but I can't,' sighed Elizabeth. 'There's just too much to do upstairs, and the new maid is coming in to see if we like her or not, and Lord! It's hot. Everyone in town will be in a state of inelegance. I think I'll put it off until the weather breaks.'

Fanny looked out of the window. Yes, it was going to be even warmer than yesterday. She saw the trees of the avenue through a sort of shimmer of heat, even though it wasn't yet ten o'clock.

'Well,' she said, with careful casualness, 'if no one else wants the carriage today, I wonder if perhaps Anna and I borrow it.'

'What for?' asked Elizabeth at once. 'Can't you girls stay here and help me?'

Fanny hadn't a clear plan in mind. But she just felt, deep down, that she couldn't bear another day here in the park. She needed to go and start investigating what had happened to Mr Drummer, and to do that she needed a means of escape.

Aunt Jane was safely hidden behind her own newspaper. But to Fanny's surprise, she now lowered it.

'I think the girls *should* go into town,' Aunt Jane said, 'and I think I'll go with them. I have one or two errands at the shops.'

'Oh, please yourselves,' cried Elizabeth. 'Don't say I didn't warn you it will be horribly hot. And don't leave until Mrs Sackree's list is written down, for you must take it with you.'

It was nearly two hours later that their ordinary dresses had been exchanged for clean white muslins, and that Mrs Sackree's list had at last been produced.

Fanny was waiting in the carriage when Aunt Jane joined her, wearing a giant straw bonnet like a governess's.

'Where *is* that girl?' asked Aunt Jane, meaning Anna, fanning herself with the shopping list. The post-chaise had arrived after breakfast, but brought with it only disappointment. There was no sign of the longed-for letter from Uncle James.

Fanny leaned forward. 'Aunt Jane,' she said, confidentially. 'Anna and I have decided something. We've decided to investigate the case of Mr Dominic Drummer. We think there's a mystery there, and we want to solve it.'

'Good for you, Fanny!' her aunt said at once. 'And if you ask her nicely, your wise old aunt will help you too.'

Before Fanny could reply, Anna came running out of the front door, carrying her parasol, and the carriage moved off.

Fanny's hot head ached, in anticipation of the cooler air beneath the trees. She began to think how exactly to start the investigation.

'... and you won't need your parasol where we're going,' Aunt Jane was saying.

'Aren't we going straight to Market Street?' Fanny asked. That was where the haberdasher's was.

'No,' said Aunt Jane, shifting her bonnet back a bit on her head so that she could see the girls better. 'We are going to begin your investigation. We're going to the House of Correction!'

'But, Aunt Jane!' Fanny cried, aghast. 'Papa would never allow that!'

Aunt Jane sighed.

'You don't understand the role of an aunt, Fanny,' she said. 'It is to *break the rules*. And sometimes to do the things that parents won't or can't do. You girls *should* see the House of Correction, for one day, as I've told you, you will be heroines, and you can't just stick to the goody-goody world of the drawing room and tea parties. You need to see and know more than that to become heroines. It's part of growing up.'

With that, Aunt Jane clamped her jaw shut, and fell to looking out of the window.

Fanny turned to Anna, seated on her other side, unsure whether to protest or not. She felt that she ought to, but she feared that Anna would be all too keen to do exactly what Aunt Jane had suggested.

It was true. Anna was wriggling about with delight.

'Aunt Jane!' she said. 'I always knew you were butter *and* jam *and* cream, all at once. Let's go to prison, and look for Mr Drummer!'

She spotted Fanny's frown.

'Oh, Fan,' she said. 'Come on. It won't kill you. And you might even find a charming gaoler to marry!'

Fanny could not help but snort at Anna's commitment to the idea of hunting for a husband. She subsided into thoughtful silence.

Was it possible that she could ever be a heroine, like Aunt Jane wanted? It seemed unlikely. Even her clever aunt might sometimes be wrong.

But yesterday Fanny had confronted her father, something she'd never done before, and now, this very minute, she was boldly doing something of which she was sure he would disapprove.

Fanny decided that there might be hope for her yet.

Chapter 16

The House of Correction, Canterbury

The House of Correction! Fanny had seen the gigantic stone gate before, many times, on the road into town. It stood close to the edge of Canterbury, in the streets where the working people lived, not among the fine mansions that sprang up as you got nearer the centre.

She'd certainly never thought she might one day go through that gateway herself.

'Aunt Jane?'

Her aunt was still looking out of the window, thinking her own thoughts, and Fanny had to ask twice before she responded.

'Aunt Jane, have you been to a House of Correction before?'

'Yes,' her aunt said, turning back towards the girls. 'I think it's important to see … all sides of life. Not just what happens inside the fence of Godmersham Park.'

Anna and Fanny looked at each other. Yes, there was perhaps more to the world than they knew. What happened at Godmersham and the other big houses nearby had seemed exciting and fulfilling enough … until now.

'I visit from time to time,' Aunt Jane explained, 'just to keep an eye on things. I have my own favourites among the prisoners.'

'No!' said Anna. 'What a mysterious person you are. Do Uncle Edward and Aunt Elizabeth know that you come here?'

Aunt Jane was looking at Anna very hard over the tops of her spectacles.

'I'm not sure that they do know, Anna,' she said. 'But then there are a lot of things in the world with which Fanny's parents aren't familiar. And here we are.'

The carriage was jolting through the forbidding archway, and across what seemed to be abnormally bumpy cobblestones.

'Now remember, girls,' said Aunt Jane, with her hand

on the door. 'You are *heroines*. You are here to see the world, and to learn what it's like.'

Fanny's heart seemed to be hammering away under her bodice as she stepped down from the carriage. This was a strange place to find herself, but very soon she might see Mr Dominic Drummer!

Perhaps she could even help him, and perhaps he would be grateful. And perhaps she, too, would enjoy solving mysteries, just like the real-life thief-takers her aunt loved so much to read about in the newspapers.

The courtyard was enclosed on all sides by walls with row upon row of windows.

Fanny saw at once, with a shiver, that in each window there were bars.

A man in a dirty suit was coming forward to meet them.

'They're used to the gentry coming to visit,' her aunt was explaining, 'to entertain themselves by laughing at the lunatics. He will think you've come in the same spirit.'

The doorkeeper was now bowing, in an embarrassingly cringing way. Fanny saw although he was pretending not to, he was holding out his hand quite brazenly for money.

Aunt Jane briskly did the business, letting a coin or two drop from her gloved fingers into his.

'Much obliged, I'm sure, madam,' he said, and pocketed the money swiftly. 'This way, if you please, young ladies. We will show you some good fun.'

He smiled, but his grin looked out of place on his greasy, crumpled-looking face. He held out a hand, as if he wanted Fanny to take it so that he could help her. She pretended she hadn't seen.

As they crossed the yard, Fanny became aware of the noises of the place. She could hear hoots, and yells, and … was that a scream? Were people screaming here?

Then her heart nearly stopped.

For a second, Fanny's eyes had rested on the bars of one of the windows.

And just for a second, she had seen those bars clutched, no, seized, in some kind of desperation, by a set of grimy knuckles within. Then there was a sickening howl, and the knuckles disappeared, as if their possessor had been dragged downwards and inwards away from the light.

What sort of place was this?

Anna answered the very question that had been in Fanny's mind.

'This is no place for Mr Drummer!' she said angrily.

'My uncle is greatly at fault for having abandoned him here, to be treated like a common criminal.'

Following Aunt Jane inside, Fanny's eyes took a little while to get used to the dim light. The floor seemed to be covered with a mixture of old straw, dirt and strange, horrible pools of wetness. Along the wall were what at first appeared to be animals, lined up like the cows in the barn at Godmersham when they were waiting to be milked.

To her horror, as her eyes grew accustomed to the dark, Fanny made out that they weren't cattle, but men. Poor miserable men, their skin glimmering with sweat and their clothes – where they had clothes – in rags. There was a dreadful clinking sound, and Fanny saw that each one of them was chained by the arm or leg to his section of wall.

With Fanny's entrance, they started up a kind of hooting and jeering, and rattling of their chains in a jangling chorus.

The slimy servant was once again standing before them in a deep bow.

'Dear young ladies!' he said. 'Welcome to the Clink. They welcome you with the clinking of their chains. Now, would you like to see some of our lunatics dancing?'

With that, he whisked out from behind his back

something that Fanny identified, to her horror, as a riding whip.

But Aunt Jane was replying.

'No, not at all,' she said. 'Take us at once to the interview room, if you please. We wish to see a young man admitted here a few weeks ago.'

The man did not answer or move.

Then Fanny noticed that his dirt-seamed palm was outstretched once again.

Once again, her aunt dealt with the request, and they moved on through the fetid gloom.

Anna's face looked very pale, and Fanny thought her cousin might be sick. She stopped abruptly. 'Aunt Jane,' Anna said, 'how can Uncle Edward be a magistrate, yet allow this place to be run like this?'

'Different institutions,' Aunt Jane said. 'This place is run by its governors. And the courts by the magistrates. And sometimes people fall between the cracks. That's why we are here! To investigate a possible miscarriage of justice.'

She gathered her skirts, but now the prison warder was the one who refused to move.

'Are you quite sure you wish to introduce the young ladies to one of the criminals?' he said. 'It's not usual.'

'Pray fetch Mr Dominic Drummer,' said Aunt Jane, crisply, 'and bring him to us. Without delay!'

She stalked right up to the man, standing almost on his toes. Aunt Jane was tall enough to tower over him menacingly, and she looked as skinny and sticklike as a witch.

That seemed to do the trick. He took them through a door with a little iron grille, as if to allow the warders sight and sound of any interview taking place within.

There were few objects in the stuffy cell beyond it, just a crude table, illuminated by hot shafts of sunlight. Within these beams of light, motes of dust, or maybe little gnats, moved about like frogs swimming in a pond.

Anna removed her bonnet and sat down. Some damp strands of dark hair clung to her forehead.

'That door isn't locked, is it?' Fanny asked. But neither of the others answered, and she felt silly. Of course it wasn't locked. They were here of their own accord. They were free to leave.

But the very idea of being locked into this terrible place as a punishment once again made her stomach do a flip-flop. What if her father knew she'd come here?

They all waited.

Then, all at a rush, the door opened, and in through it very quickly, as if shoved, came the person they'd wanted to see.

Mr Drummer stood swaying before them, pushing a long and unwashed fringe back from his forehead and tugging down the rolled-up sleeves of his shirt. Fanny saw that his skin had taken on the grey pallor of the place, and the people in it.

He looked so grimy, and unhappy, and so different from what she'd expected, that it shocked her. And, unlike the previous times they'd met, he simply wouldn't meet her eye. If anything, he looked horrified to see her.

Aunt Jane spoke, kindly and calmly. She explained that his plight had only recently come to her own attention and that of her nieces, and naturally as his friends they felt a special interest in his case, and would he mind explaining what it was all about?

Mr Drummer looked at the floor in mute agony.

He murmured something, and tugged again at his grubby shirt.

Aunt Jane obviously understood what he said, and spoke more urgently.

'Mr Drummer! This is not the time to worry about propriety, or even the state of your linen. To put it frankly, we fear that you've been placed here unjustly, and that

122

your own modesty has prevented you from asking your friends for help.'

A painful blush rose up the young man's neck. He needed a shave, Fanny saw. It must be part of the cause of his shame.

She saw that Mr Drummer was torn between pride, and wanting them to go away, and desperate longing for a bit of sympathy.

She found her two hands were wringing each other, entirely of their own accord, something she'd never noticed them doing before.

Mr Drummer shuffled his weight from one foot to the other, blushing and blinking, and Fanny had to look away. It was unbearable to see him like this.

Finally, very reluctantly, he sat himself down at the table.

'That is something like the truth,' he admitted. 'And you, Miss Austen, have been far too good to me. It is to you I owed my place at Godmersham, and I could not bear to inconvenience you or embarrass you by letting you know what had happened.'

'Let that be over!' cried Aunt Jane, perhaps more passionate than Fanny had ever seen her.

The warder looked in through the hole in the door at the sound of the raised voice.

'All well, all well,' Aunt Jane said hurriedly.

Mr Drummer stared hard at his hands on the table.

'The thing is,' he began, 'I think I am guilty. I am guilty as charged. But I really don't understand why.'

'What happened in the shop?' Aunt Jane asked him gently. 'Take me through it step by step. I have some experience of thief-taking.'

There was no time for Fanny to catch Anna's eye in surprise at this revelation. There was simply too much to take in.

'Well, I bought my gloves,' he said uncertainly, 'with the money that you yourself, Miss Austen, were kind enough to give me in advance of my stipend being paid. Mr Austen,' he said, mumbling in Fanny's direction, 'meant to do it, but he has so many matters to consider, so much business on his mind, that I didn't like to ask.'

'Stop thinking of everyone's fine feelings,' Aunt Jane commanded him. 'The story, if you please.'

But Fanny hung her head. Her father had forgotten to give the young man his stipend! And he'd had no ready money!

'So, I came out of the shop, with my gloves wrapped up in a paper package. And then, the woman came after me, and she said that she was missing a piece of valuable lace, and that she thought I had slipped it into my package!'

'And had you?' Anna asked. The sound of her voice surprised Fanny. Her attention had been so focused upon Dominic Drummer, and upon remembering how well shaped his jaw was, that she'd forgotten Anna was present.

'Of course not!' Mr Drummer said.

Yet he sounded bemused rather than indignant.

'But this is the part I don't understand,' he continued. 'Of course I didn't steal the lace, the very thought is ridiculous. I didn't even do up the package. She did it for me. But she was most forceful, and she insisted that I go back into the shop. Then she insisted on opening up the package. I didn't object because I knew – believed – that of course there had been some mistake, and that she must have confused me with someone else.'

Fanny could easily imagine his courtesy, his willingness to please, perhaps his embarrassment on the shop assistant's behalf at the mistake he thought she must have made.

'And then?'

Aunt Jane spoke, as his words had petered out.

Mr Drummer shook his head from side to side in wonderment, as if he could still not believe it.

125

'Well, that's the strange thing. There were the gloves, just as I thought, but there too inside the brown paper was a piece of lace, fine Brussels stuff, you know. She said it was worth forty shillings! And she insisted at once on calling the constables, and the other people in the shop looked at me, and they thought I was a thief, and ...'

His humiliation was palpable. It almost coloured the air.

'And you never once spoke up for yourself?' Aunt Jane asked gently. 'You never shouted, or said that there had been some mistake?'

He gradually lifted his head until his eyes met hers. Fanny could see beads of perspiration on his forehead, dampening his hair.

'No,' he said. 'Because the evidence was there. Before my eyes. In a fit of madness, or forgetfulness, or something, I must have done it. I must have stolen the lace.'

Chapter 17

The breakfast table, Godmersham Park

During the carriage ride home, a silence fell upon the three of them. It had all been so unexpected. Fanny grew conscious of an ache in her head, and Mrs Sackree's shopping not even started.

But Anna jogged Fanny's arm.

'Do you know what I've just remembered?'

Fanny shrugged.

'I forgot about it while we were with Mr Drummer. But if my father's letter didn't come today, it must surely come tomorrow! In just twelve hours' time!'

Fanny's thoughts jerked back from the prison and the poor dirty madmen, back to the park of Godmersham and all the things which had seemed so important there. For her cousin's sake, she mustered up a smile.

Aunt Jane carried on looking inscrutably out of the window. After he'd told them his story, Fanny's aunt had promised Mr Drummer she'd try to get him moved, out of the common ward and into the gentlemen prisoners' rooms in the gaoler's house. She'd had to insist, ignoring his protestations.

'Don't,' Aunt Jane had said. 'The Austen family owe you.'

What a different world, Fanny thought, as she now rested her eyes upon the chestnut trees as they drove into the park.

Why did she have the good fortune to live here? She and her siblings, but for a twist of fate, might have been living the lives of those frightening witless creatures in the lunatic ward.

And now, at breakfast the following day, Fanny's father was talking of the haymaking, and the harvest, and how the good weather might make it a bumper year.

Fanny felt a little strange as she looked at all the rolls, the jam, the jug of cream, and the silver coffee pot on the table. This was a bumper breakfast, and no mistake, and poor Mr Drummer wouldn't be having anything like it.

She couldn't even understand why Mr Drummer was in that place. He certainly couldn't understand it himself. It was as if chance, not justice, had landed him there.

Fanny put down her half-eaten piece of toast. She remembered again his haunted face, and how ashamed he'd been of his hairy throat. She feared that her headache might come back.

But now there was a pounding of feet in the passage, and the door flew open. Anna was there, still in her dressing gown, with her hair all loose.

'Saw … the post-chaise … from my bedroom window!' she gasped. 'It's come! Open it, Uncle Edward, open it!'

She was holding a folded letter, with the red wax seal turned upwards.

Everyone at the breakfast table turned towards Fanny's father. Fanny's mother stood up, one hand on her heart, the other on Anna's shoulder, pushing her down into a chair.

'Carefully now!' she was saying. 'Remember to breathe, dear Anna!'

But Elizabeth's own face was pink as well. The same excitement must be fizzing inside everyone's stomach.

Fanny looked solemnly at her cousin. Anna's future, Anna's fate, might be decided in that letter. Had Uncle James allowed her to become engaged?

Fanny's father picked up a butter knife to open the letter's seal. It was a used, greasy one, but not even his wife had the heart to tell him off.

He read to the very end before saying anything.

'Well?'

Fanny's mother almost shrieked the word.

A big slow smile spread across Edward's face.

Fanny noticed that he was enjoying this.

'My brother James has … given his consent,' he said at last. 'He takes into account our wishes, as dear friends of his niece. So Anna is to be Mrs Terry! We're going to have our first family wedding!'

With that the room seemed almost to go up in flames. Brothers and sisters were hugging Anna, and whooping, and Mrs Sackree was looking round the door to find out what all the uproar was.

But Anna herself said nothing, and her face was blank. Fanny's father still sat there, smiling, looking again at his brother's letter and rereading it.

Anna, Fanny noticed, was watching him intently, even while Marianne and Louie climbed all over her.

'I must see what I can do for the young man,' Fanny's father said, at last, as if to himself.

He scarcely seemed to notice that, at that moment, his niece flew up out of her seat and ran round the table to give him a smacking kiss.

'An Austen engagement!' crowed Elizabeth. 'And many more yet to come, girls,' she said to Lizzie and Marianne.

Fanny looked down at her napkin. Her mother seemed not to have remembered, at this moment, that Fanny herself might have wanted, even expected, to have been the first Miss Austen engaged.

But now here was Anna, throwing her arms round Fanny's neck and giving her a great big squeeze.

Soon their mother was ordering the carriage, and trying to organise everyone into getting dressed. There were calls to be paid on all her friends, to spread the news.

Elizabeth bustled herself right out of the room, while Fanny's father turned to the rest of the post. Aunt Jane seized the newspaper, smiling at Anna as she sat down.

'Have you got your *heart's desire* at last, dear Anna?' she asked, comfortably. 'I am very happy for you.'

'Oh *yes*,' cried Anna, and Fanny could see that tears were glinting in her eyes. But Anna's face didn't seem full of joy. If anything, Fanny would have described her expression as relieved.

Chapter 18

Aunt Jane's bedroom, Godmersham Park

Anna would be busy for the rest of the morning, Fanny suspected, being paraded round the house by her aunt Elizabeth and reintroduced to all the servants as the future Mrs Terry. Neither of them would be needing Fanny. It was a lonely feeling.

When breakfast was finished, though, Aunt Jane gave Fanny one of her sharp nods. As if by common consent, they slipped upstairs and into Aunt Jane's room.

'So!' said Aunt Jane, throwing herself down on the sofa. She kicked her slippers off her bony feet, propped them up on a cushion and relaxed her long body as if exhausted. 'What a great deal of emotion!'

To Fanny's surprise, she felt her eyes pricking with tears.

'Oh, Fanny,' said her aunt, sitting up again. 'You and Anna really are irresistible. Look at you! Remember how desperate you were, a few hours ago, for this very thing to come to pass?'

'Well, yes,' Fanny conceded. 'But I'm not ... feeling entirely right. Ever since we went to the House of Correction, I've felt hot and odd.'

'It's partly the weather,' said her aunt, fanning herself with a piece of scribbled-on paper. 'These have been torrid times both indoors and out. But look, the chestnuts are beginning to turn. There's cooler weather coming.'

Fanny glanced out of Aunt Jane's window. Yes, up here amongst the leaves of the crowns of the trees she could see that they were just on the brink of turning golden.

Soon they'd fall, Fanny thought. When that happened, she would have been out in society for a whole six months, yet not a single step closer to being married.

But Aunt Jane hadn't finished. 'And,' she was saying, 'I wouldn't be surprised if Anna's engagement makes you perhaps feel a little ... cheated? Put out?'

Fanny was so glad that her aunt had said it.

'Of course, I'm happy Anna's getting married,' she said, in a rush, 'but what about … what about me?'

Aunt Jane propped herself on an elbow.

'Come here, Fanny,' she said. 'That's right, sit down there on the carpet against the sofa, and I can mop your fevered brow.'

Soon her aunt's paper-wafting was creating a gentle breeze over Fanny's throbbing forehead.

'You have been like two peas in a pod,' her aunt was saying, in a faraway voice. 'You have been like two halves of a whole, ever since you were born to my two brothers in exactly the same year. No wonder you feel that you're being ripped asunder.'

'But I'm supposed to *want* us to be ripped asunder, and married, and to have homes of our own!'

'Yes,' said her aunt. 'You're supposed to.' But then she said no more.

The silence lengthened. It was like a pool of water. Fanny felt an urge to drop in a pebble, to ask something she'd long wanted to know.

'Aunt Jane,' she said, 'why haven't *you* ever got married?'

Her aunt had stretched back out on the chaise again. Fanny noticed that her toes began to twitch about, very slightly, like a cat's tail when you stroked its fur the wrong way.

'A number of reasons,' Aunt Jane said to the ceiling. 'Firstly, I prefer being peaceful and lazy. Look at your mother; how hard she has to work, running the house, looking after you children, and her niece too, giving, giving, giving all the time.'

Fanny raised her eyebrows. To her it seemed that her mother was more of a taker. She took away fun, *frequently* took away books, saying that Fanny was reading too much, took ill-aimed smacks at her children when they acted up.

'Then,' Aunt Jane continued, 'I never met a man I liked well enough to give up my freedom to do various things which, ahem, wouldn't be possible if I were married.'

Fanny sat up and turned to look at her aunt.

'You mean, you never met a man you liked more than us, your family? I suppose Anna must prefer Mr Terry to me,' she said sadly.

'Well,' said Aunt Jane, suddenly growing serious instead of ruminative, and engaging Fanny's eyes with her own. 'I sincerely hope that she does.'

What could Aunt Jane mean? Did she wonder whether Anna really loved Mr Terry?

Fanny didn't often see her aunt's eyes, but now they were big and brown and boring right into her.

'Has she spoken much of Mr Terry to you, Fanny?'

When Aunt Jane asked you a direct question, it was impossible not to answer.

Fanny knew that there was a right and a wrong answer to this, and she wished that she could give a different reply. She broke her aunt's gaze, but felt compelled to speak.

'Well, no, not that much,' she admitted. 'She has, in general terms, you know, she's told me things he's said to her, his house, his family, and so on. But she hasn't said much about his character.'

Aunt Jane was leaning forward.

'It's all been very quick,' she said. 'Hasn't it? You and I, Fanny, must watch out for Anna. Perhaps she doesn't know this young man terribly well, and perhaps he doesn't know her. And as you and I both know, she can be so passionate, and so … well, to be blunt about it, she can be *difficult*. We must try to help her.'

Fanny nodded, and relaxed against the side of the sofa. She folded her arms upon it and rested her face on them. Of course Aunt Jane understood.

'It's true,' Fanny said quietly, into the darkness. 'My

137

cousin is in love with having her own way. Perhaps she wanted her own way as much as she wanted him.'

'It's possible,' said Aunt Jane. 'Now tell me something else, Fanny. Is there anyone who's special to you? More than just friends?'

'No, no,' said Fanny, quickly, dismayed. She knew of course Aunt Jane was asking about Mr Drummer. But she'd been told so often and so clearly that he was not an option for her. 'Of course not.'

'Well,' said her aunt, 'we'll see.'

It was almost as if she didn't believe Fanny. But to Fanny's relief, she let the matter drop.

'We shall find out very soon,' Aunt Jane continued, 'what Mr Terry is really like when he comes to visit.'

'Is he coming here?'

'Yes,' her aunt said. 'My brother has invited him. So we have lots of excitement ahead. Which means, my dear,' she said, gathering herself up in a manner that Fanny knew was a dismissal, 'that I need my room to myself for a while, to be getting on with, well, my business.'

Fanny left, half satisfied. If she had a pact with Aunt Jane to watch over her cousin and to help her, then perhaps all could be well.

Chapter 19

The front door, Godmersham Park

A few days later, the weather had well and truly broken. The grey sky was almost a relief after the relentless sun.

Letters had been flying between Kent and Hampshire. Fanny had written to her uncle James and aunt Mary, saying, or in fact exaggerating, how much she was looking forward to being a bridesmaid. Mr Terry had written to say that he would like very much to come to stay at Godmersham to meet his fiancée's Kentish family. And Anna had written to everyone she knew in the whole world, announcing her joy at being engaged even though she was only just sixteen.

Fanny had read these letters through, at Anna's

request, to correct the spelling mistakes, and privately thought it would have been more attractive if Anna had left out her age. Whenever she spotted an error, Fanny corrected it with a sharp little slash of her pen.

At length, the day came upon which Mr Terry was expected. There was definitely a September nip and the promise of apples in the air. Fanny's father had sent the Godmersham carriage to bring Mr Terry home from the Star Inn, where the public stagecoach dropped its passengers.

The family waited on the gravel outside the house. Marianne had even made a canvas banner, which read, in painted letters, *Welcome to Godmeshm*.

Anna had made the error of laughing at the mis-spelling, but Aunt Jane had said it was a perfectly comprehensible abbreviation of the name of the house, and that if Mr Terry couldn't work out what it said then he was a sorry stick.

The wait seemed interminable. Fanny's sisters occu-pied the time by discussing what they would wear as bridesmaids, and whether their brothers would be pages.

'Boys!' said Elizabeth. 'Surely for once you can polish your shoe buckles and behave nicely for your cousin's wedding?'

'Not – polish – anything – for – a – *girl*,' said William, although he was barely able to speak. He had hurt his teeth trying to find out if gravel was edible.

Fanny noticed that just two people were quiet. Anna didn't have much to say, even about the subject of her own wedding dress. *She's* nervous, Fanny thought. And Aunt Jane, too, was keeping her own counsel, standing with her arms folded. But there was nothing unexpected about that.

'Will he *never* come?' Fanny sighed to Aunt Jane. 'I can't bear it!'

But even as she spoke, there was a shout, as if the stable boys had spotted the carriage coming along the drive. Everyone fell silent. Fanny saw her brother Edward sticking out his chest and grasping the lapels of his coat, in imitation of their father. His performance as a miniature lord of the manor made her smile.

And then the carriage was in sight, and the coachman James was calling 'whoa' to the horses, and the whole equipage was grinding to a halt amid a spray of fine gravel and a misting of fine rain.

There was a pause, then the carriage door opened.

An unremarkable man in a black suit, rather stooped and elderly, emerged. He made two unsuccessful attempts to get his hat on to his head. He stood there with his back towards them all, fumbling to fix a pince-nez to his nose.

'Oh, where is Mr Terry?' Marianne cried in agony. 'Why hasn't he come? Did he miss the stagecoach?'

The man still stood there, confused, as if he didn't know quite what to do.

Fanny glanced at Anna, and saw that her cousin's face was set.

Slowly Fanny realised what was happening. Mr Terry couldn't see without his spectacles.

Anna swallowed hard, and stepped forward.

'This way,' she called. 'Here we all are!'

He turned at her voice, fixing his spectacles more firmly to his nose and snatching off his hat to bow low, lower … Fanny was afraid that he might fall over and hurt himself, so awkward did he seem.

Anna hooked her elbow defiantly through the man's black-coated arm, lurched him back to his feet and marched him towards her aunt and uncle. There was a bright social smile on her face.

'This,' she said, 'is Mr Terry. May I have the honour, Uncle Edward and Aunt Elizabeth, to present my fiancé?'

From the flurried warmth of their greetings, Fanny could tell that her father and mother had, like Marianne, not realised that this … man … could possibly be Anna's future husband.

Fanny turned away, to spare herself the sight of her family's false enthusiasm.

As she did so, she saw that Aunt Jane's piercing gaze was taking in every detail of Mr Terry's reception. There was no embarrassment on her aunt's face, just fascination.

Fanny gave an exasperated shrug of her shoulders. Aunt Jane seemed to *enjoy* the situations which mortified Fanny most deeply.

'Not quite what we expected,' Aunt Jane hissed in her ear.

Fanny began to brace herself for the moment when she'd have to speak to him. Looking again, she realised that Mr Terry wasn't so very old after all; it was his stoop that made him seem so. So too did his spindly black calves in their black stockings.

Anna really must get him to trim his eyebrows, Fanny said to herself. *They're so tufty!*

How different he was from the hero of a romantic story!

Anna was now bringing Mr Terry along the line of Fanny's siblings. To Fanny's horror, Marianne was staring at him open-mouthed, her banner drooping in her hand.

'But he's so *old*!' came Marianne's all-too-audible hiss.

And now here was Mr Terry himself taking her hand, and saying how very pleased he was to meet Anna's favourite cousin again, and that there was so close a connection between them that they were practically sisters.

Fanny said how pleased she was too, the words coming out mechanically, almost as if she were following a script.

Then Anna turned to take Mr Terry into the house, the pair of them walking through the rain towards the door self-consciously, heads lowered, not talking.

Fanny herself stepped back with exaggerated courtesy to make room for them to pass. Oh, but this was a damp beginning indeed.

Chapter 20

The hay barn, Godmersham Park

Anna spent the afternoon showing Mr Terry the house, and then, beneath umbrellas, the gardens. Next, Mr Terry was summoned into the library for a conference with Fanny's father, while Fanny's mother bustled Anna upstairs for a matronly discussion of housekeeping.

Fanny was left stranded in the hall, wondering what to do. How could she please her mother, who seemed to be acting more like Anna's mother now? Fanny had an idea. Surely her mother would be pleased if she took the younger girls out of the way.

'Children!' she shouted, in her best imitation of Elizabeth. 'We'll go out to the barn and jump into the hay.'

Her words with met with a ragged cheer, and the thunder of small feet.

Bond the farmer would be furious, she knew, and subsequently her father would be cross. But the rain had set in, and if possible the mansion should be kept quiet so that – in Aunt Jane's words – Mr Terry would not think he had come to stay in a madhouse.

There could well be a lot of days like this ahead, Fanny brooded, picking her way across the damp ground towards the barn. It was awful being neither one of the children, nor the grown-ups, but in between.

She sat mooching by herself on a hay bale, stirring only to give the occasional yell at Louie and Marianne to keep well away from the scythe hung up on the barn's wall. And then she had to reassure the little girls that their brothers were only shouting 'Rats! Rats!' in the yard outside in order needlessly to frighten them.

As Fanny leaned back again on the bale, she felt the prickling of it through her stockings. Silk ones, not cotton, put on in Mr Terry's honour. Had they been worth it?

He really did look ever so much like a black beetle. And his smile had revealed his greyish teeth. She tried to imagine him kissing Anna. It was horrible.

'Fanny?'

It was a mournful little voice from behind her. Marianne had straws and wisps of hay sticking out of her hair, and there was a stain down the front of her gown.

'Oh, Marianne, why didn't you put your apron on, silly?' Fanny asked, pulling her sister down to join her on the bale. Marianne's shoulders felt comfortingly warm. The little ones had been running about and destroying hay bales like a vengeful army.

Fanny now saw that Marianne's face was troubled, almost comically sad beneath her hay-filled hair.

'What is it, sweets?' she asked, expecting a story of a sore knee, or a cruel brother.

'Fanny,' Marianne asked again, and there was a little quiver in her voice, 'is Anna really going to marry that man?'

Fanny was taken aback. She'd assumed that her fears and hopes for Anna would be invisible to the little girls. And yet everything, it seemed, was transparent.

'Well, what's wrong with him? He's a respectable man, Marianne, and likely to be kind to Anna, and to have a nice house for her to live in, and, oh, and of course she must really like him too.'

Marianne's neck drooped.

'But he's so, well, boring,' Fanny's sister complained.

147

'He never said anything at all, all through tea, except to give his annoying laugh!'

Fanny had to admit that Mr Terry had an unfortunate habit of tittering pointlessly whenever he was asked a question. But whatever her personal doubts, she had a duty to Anna.

'Marianne,' she said seriously. 'You don't know him yet. Anna does, and she must love him. She thinks his jokes are funny, and so on, and if Anna loves somebody, so must we too.'

Marianne frowned, and Fanny could see thoughts passing across her pale little face one after another, like clouds scudding across the sky on a windy day.

'But, Fanny!' she said at last. 'I don't believe that Anna *does* love Mr Terry!'

Fanny's own heart fell. Could Marianne also have seen what she herself suspected?

'I think,' Marianne continued boldly, 'she's ashamed of him.'

A cold feeling grew inside Fanny, chilling the air in her lungs and creeping out along her limbs.

Yes, it was true. Anna didn't seem at all happy, or proud, or confident of Mr Terry. It was almost, now that he was actually here at Godmersham, as if she were dourly determined to make the best of him.

Feeling guilty even as she did it, Fanny whispered consoling nothings to Marianne, telling her that of course Anna would be happy, and pushing her off to play.

But once her sister was shoving and whooping once again, Fanny fell to playing with a strand of straw, folding it, pushing it and pulling it in her hands, endlessly, relentlessly.

Yes, although Marianne was just a baby, she had spoken truthfully. Fanny herself must see Anna privately, and try to find out more. Was it really worth putting up with a man with grey teeth, just to say that you were married?

Chapter 21

Fanny's bedroom, Godmersham Park

Dinner was such agony.

Each time Mr Terry spoke, everyone else, Mr and Mrs Austen, Fanny and Anna, even the children, fell suddenly silent, as if to pay him the courteous attention his words must surely deserve.

Yet when he opened his mouth, what came out was so stilted and dreary it was as if he was deliberately trying to make a bad impression.

'It's a shame the weather has broken!' Fanny's father began jovially.

'Indeed,' said Mr Terry.

Everyone waited for him to go on, but it seemed that even commenting on the weather was beyond him.

'The young ladies will be sorry to be denied the use of the park,' Mr Austen persevered.

'I'm sure the young ladies will make good use of the time to read their Bibles instead,' Mr Terry offered up, after one of his nervous giggles.

'Oh, but my girls love to romp outside!' said Mrs Austen. 'Are you fond of walking yourself, Mr Terry?'

'Not particularly,' he said.

'How do you get around your parish?'

Mr Terry looked daggers at Marianne, who had spoken.

'I have, as yet, no parish, Miss … erm, Miss Marianne,' he said. 'I am still a curate.'

'But how old are you?' Marianne cried. 'You look much too old to be a curate! They're generally *young* men.'

'Marianne!'

The chorus from the other Austens was deafening. Amid it all Mr Terry sat sweating, and twitching his eye, and making a strange little jerky movement of his head.

Fanny noticed that he even ate clumsily, spilling his soup down his dingy black coat, then frantically dabbing the stain with a napkin.

Poor man, she said to herself severely. *He obviously only has one suit. But that's not a crime! Anna's always*

saying that here at Godmersham we attach too much
importance to material things.

There was a squeak as her brother George succeeded in kicking Marianne into silence under the table.

'Do you ride to hounds, Mr Terry?' George asked, picking up the conversational ball. George's main interest in life was horses, with dogs coming a close second.

'Certainly not!' said Mr Terry, shocked. 'I disapprove most sincerely of a hunting parson.'

Fanny caught George's reproachful glance at Anna for having chosen such a useless husband.

'Oh, but really, Mr Terry,' her father was saying. 'It's God's duty for every human being to enjoy himself, you know. Or herself. I hold that as a divine command.'

'Enjoyment,' replied Anna's fiancé, looking down at his plate, 'takes no high place on my list of endeavours in life.'

Fanny could not help but catch Anna's eye. Her cousin shrugged, and looked quickly away. She must have seen what Fanny's eyes could not hide: her consternation.

Hours and hours later, it seemed, Fanny and Anna were in Fanny's room, getting ready for bed. Fanny thought that there'd never been such a long evening at Godmersham Park. When Anna came to stay, the long late-summer twilights usually flew past, in charades or singing if not in laughing and gossiping.

'Everyone was too much on their best behaviour,' Anna was explaining as she twisted her hair into a rope. She was going to share Fanny's bed, as she'd vacated the guest room so that Mr Terry could have it. 'He was intimidated.'

Fanny sighed. She could see what Anna was saying. The Austens were so numerous and boisterous, so sure of themselves. But could the man who was worthy of Anna have so little self-confidence?

'Marianne was incredibly rude!' Fanny eventually pronounced, having searched for at least something she could say that was true. She reached over Anna's shoulder and tipped the looking glass to reflect them both. Shadowy, illuminated, their two faces glimmered back, one dark-haired, one so fair she was almost ghostly.

'He was happy to see *you* again, Fanny!' Anna said to their joint reflection.

'And I ...'

Fanny faltered, braced herself, went on.

'And I was happy to see him. I was pleased when he told me we were like sisters.'

Anna picked up the tail of her hair and gave it a few savage blows with Fanny's hairbrush.

'I wish we really were sisters,' she muttered. 'Not least because then Uncle Edward would give me lots of money, and then I could marry a lord after all.'

'Can your father …'

It was difficult to ask, as Anna was so prickly on the subject.

'Can Uncle James give you nothing at all? To be married on, I mean?'

Anna turned away and stared at the floor. Then she seemed to make a special effort. Turning back, she smoothed Fanny's own hair with the brush. It was a soothing feeling.

'No. Nothing. I'm sure my uncle Edward will be very kind,' she said. 'But it gets boring having to be grateful the whole time.'

It was awkward. Things had never been this awkward between them before. Fanny's heart bled inside her. It ached for her proud, poor cousin.

'Oh, Anna!' she said all in a rush, putting her hand on Anna's shoulder. 'Are you really sure, absolutely really sure, that he's the right man for you? You seem so … different from each other,' Fanny added. 'And it's for life, you know, not just for a dancing season.'

Anna shoved Fanny away, almost brutally.

'Oh yes,' she said sourly. 'He's poor. There's no getting

away from that. There's no getting away from the fact that he's thirty years old, and doesn't have a parish, and wouldn't be good enough for a Miss Austen of Godmersham.'

'That's not what I meant,' said Fanny, in some desperation. But it was too late.

Anna's voice was rising in pitch, and her words were punctuated by ragged little gasps.

'But, Fanny,' she continued, throwing down the hairbrush, 'he's *good enough for me*. He's going to take me away from horrible Steventon, and my horrible stepmother, and my horrible life there, and that must be enough. Now go and take your *pity* somewhere else.'

With that Anna flounced up from the dressing stool, threw herself into the bed and pulled the blanket round her shoulders, staring at the wall, as if having taken a vow to say nothing more.

There was a sharp squall of rain against the windowpane as Fanny blew out the candle and crept slowly in the dark to the bed.

She sat down on the edge of it and let her slippers fall off her feet. She took in a breath, ready to say that of course she didn't mean to criticise, of course she understood Anna's situation.

But once again her mind filled with the thought of Mr

Terry's tufty old-man eyebrows, and the hairs she'd seen poking out of his nostrils. Anna was only just sixteen! She would have to spend so much of her life with him!

Fanny reached down for her slippers, straightening them, lining them up ready for the morning.

She looked over at Anna's stiff shoulder.

There was a long pause. Fanny's eyes strayed back to the dark shape of her shoes. No, she just couldn't find the words.

Eventually, a tear slipped silently out of Fanny's eye, and down her cheek. It was a long time before she got properly into the bed, and even longer before she could get off to sleep.

Chapter 22

The breakfast table, Godmersham Park

When Fanny opened her eyes, she saw that Anna was up already and sitting by the window. She was looking moodily out at the park, twisting, always twisting her hair.

Fanny brought over a shawl, her favourite one in pink and green. She did not like to lend it to anyone.

'Here,' she said. 'It's chilly.'

Anna stared at her blankly and said nothing.

Fanny turned away, the shawl awkward in her hands. She once again felt tears prick.

But then she felt something different in her stomach, something hot and roiling.

Was it anger?

Yes, it was. There was no need for Anna to be so hostile. Fanny wrapped her shawl around her own shoulders and stalked right out of the bedroom. Anna was so difficult. So 'damnably difficult', as Fanny's brother Edward might say.

Where could Fanny go, dressed as she was only in her nightgown?

She went upstairs to see Louie, and was rewarded by the brightening of the little girl's face, and a 'good morning' from Mrs Sackree. *Perhaps I should come up here more often*, Fanny thought. Poor Mrs Sackree looked tired.

It could be pleasant and calm in the nursery in the early morning like this, with baby Cassie sleeping all splayed out across her cot, as if she had been poured there out of a jug.

Fanny went to pull the cord to raise the blind, and as she did so, she spotted Anna again, now mooching about by herself in the wet grass below. She must be getting her slippers soaked.

Breakfast was just as stiff as dinner had been. Fanny's eyes switched nervously between Mr Terry, who was getting crumbs down his front, and Anna, who was still wan and withdrawn.

158

She felt marginally better when Aunt Jane gave her a nod and straightened her poker-like back.

'Bear up,' Aunt Jane was saying.

The post arrived, which only reminded Fanny of the excitement in the old days when Mr Terry was just a lovely distant prospect on the horizon, and everyone was hoping that Uncle James would write agreeing to let Anna marry him.

The letter that Pemberton now presented to Fanny's father looked dull, probably a bill that would put him into a rage. But then Fanny noticed that her father had lifted his gaze from the paper, and was staring vacantly at the dripping trees outside.

'What is it, Papa?' she ventured to ask. 'Is it bad news?'

'Well,' he said, coming back to himself and giving Fanny a private grin. 'It's sad, but we'll survive. It's news of that Mr Drummer, whom you ladies like so much. He's to be tried, very soon, Mr Fortescue tells me. Of course, because the value of what he stole was forty shillings – who knew that a piece of women's frippery like lace could cost so much, heh, Mrs Austen? – his sentence might be transportation. To the colony of Australia. Sounds like an open-and-shut case.'

'Papa!' Fanny said, dismayed. 'No! There must be some mistake.'

But her father wasn't listening.

'He won't be able to come back here even if he avoids getting sent to Australia,' he continued. 'We couldn't have a parson who'd been charged with a crime.'

'Uncle Edward!'

It was Anna, on her feet. Fanny sighed. Of course, Anna had already been in a bad mood, and now her uncle had said the very thing to get her going.

'You said he *stole*,' Anna panted out, furious. 'Well, there's no evidence of that, nothing! And a citizen is innocent until proved guilty! You, a magistrate, of all people should know that!'

In her passion, she hurled her napkin down on the floor and stood there, staring at her uncle.

In the silence that followed, Fanny's father's hand crept back to the letter, as if he needed to read it again and reassure himself of the facts.

But to Fanny's surprise, Mr Terry's fluting voice cut in.

'My dear Miss Austen,' he began, faltering, but then regaining confidence. 'My dear Miss Austen, I must counsel you not to contradict your uncle. Of course, he knows best what the facts may be, and of course the full force of the law must be felt against malefactors.'

'What's a malefactor?' asked Marianne, innocently.

Fanny noticed Aunt Jane's shoulders move a tiny bit, almost as if she were swallowing a laugh.

'A malefactor,' said Mr Terry, 'is a bad person, a person beneath the notice of the Miss Austens, and it is really quite distressing and wrong for young ladies to concern themselves with such people.'

'Distressing and wrong?' cried Anna. 'What about justice? And honour? And what about this young man to whom some great evil has been done, of which my uncle *will not take the trouble to find out?*'

She had thrown back her head, and her hair had come undone. She really did look magnificent, Fanny thought. One might say that her eyes flashed. Almost like a heroine's.

Fanny noticed that Lizzie was watching Anna and Mr Terry very hard. So was Marianne. Their eyes were flicking between the two as if between the players in a game of shuttlecock. There was something she'd never felt before in that room, a real uncomfortable feeling of tension.

Mr Terry slowly stood up from the table and pompously placed the tips of his fingers upon its surface.

'I shall withdraw,' he said with ostentatious calmness, 'while Miss Anna Austen takes the time to control herself, and to recover her composure.' And he made his way towards the door in an unusually smooth version of his stumbling walk. The effect was a little spoilt by his having to turn the doorknob twice before he caught the trick of opening it.

'What's ...' began Louie.

But her mother gave her a sharp smack.

'Not now,' Elizabeth said shortly. 'Anna, Anna, it'll be all right.'

'It won't *be all right*,' Anna said crossly, 'because *none of you care*.' With that she too flounced out, this time slamming the door as hard as she could, so that its frame shook.

Fanny's father sighed.

'Well,' he said, 'she didn't stay to hear one piece of good news. A benefactor has paid for Mr Drummer to move out of the common ward and into the gaoler's house. So at least he is comfortable and getting proper food.'

'Papa!' said Lizzie. 'Was it you? That was kind.'

'No, no,' he said quickly. 'It wasn't me. I must admit, although I wouldn't say it in front of my niece, that perhaps I didn't pay as much attention as I should to the young man's predicament. Ten children, you know! All the harvest ruined in this rain. Not to mention my wife's dressmaker's bills. And no one pays me a penny for my work as a magistrate. Lord knows this system we have isn't quite fair. Now, for Heaven's sake, do stop crying, Marianne. No one is going to Australia.'

'You mean, no one is going to Australia *yet*.'

It was Aunt Jane, speaking drily as usual from her corner behind a barricade of jam jars.

Fanny's father looked hard at his sister.

'That's right, Jane,' he said evenly. 'I wonder what kind friend the young man may possess, to help him out so significantly? I thought he had no friends. It's a mystery.'

Once again Fanny felt that something strange was in the room, something unspoken, some kind of tussle of wills.

But of course, Aunt Jane couldn't have paid to get Mr Drummer into better accommodation, especially after she'd paid for Anna's stagecoach fare to Godmersham just a few weeks ago. She was an old maid. She had hardly any money.

Aunt Jane had no resources, nor did Anna, nor did Fanny herself. But she could at least do one thing.

She must find the right time to speak to Anna, and apologise, and try to console her, and to do everything she could to make it better. If only Anna would let herself be consoled.

Chapter 23

Chilham Castle, near Canterbury

And then, to cap it all, Fanny remembered with dismay, this was the very evening of the Chilham Ball.

Fanny had been looking forward to it – a ball at a real castle! – oh, for ages, even before she'd known that Anna would be staying at Godmersham and would be able to come along as well. She also had a new dress, a deep rose pink, much more exciting than the white she'd worn for her debut at the Star Inn.

But now everything was perplexing. She and Anna were still supposed to go to the ball, yet so too was Mr Terry. Fanny could not begin to imagine having a good time.

She dressed for the ball alone. Anna had secretly sloped off and got ready during teatime. Then she'd taken herself to the library, to sit there mutely with Mr Terry, each of them turning over the pages of books. Fanny knew that Mr Terry had no need to get changed himself, for he had just the one suit of clothes.

It was all so very different, Fanny felt as she descended the stairs, from the time when she and Anna had floated down on a cloud of nerves to attend their first ball back in the very early spring.

Yet when Fanny heard the dull crunch of the carriage wheels on the gravel – both carriages, for her father and mother and Mr Terry and Aunt Jane were all to be accommodated – her spirits nevertheless lifted.

It would still be a ball, after all. There was something cheerful about the very word.

Perhaps Fanny herself might meet someone perfect, someone suitable in every way. Then her duty would be done, and she could just stop worrying. The task, the decision, would be out of her hands.

On her way across the hall, Fanny mentally reviewed her partners from her last ball. Several of them were acceptable, from the point of view of her parents at least.

But none of them had Mr Drummer's diffident smile, his way of asking a question as if he really wanted to know what she thought, that special look in his eyes he used to have just for her.

It was still chilly outdoors, so Fanny skipped quickly across the forecourt, and with a jump she was in the foremost of the two carriages. Empty. Yes, she was first in, and the rest must be following.

Now she could hear running feet on the gravel – it must be Anna. To Fanny's surprise, Anna was bounding towards the vehicle, saying something to the coachman, and then banging her way in and slamming the door. Smartly and swiftly, almost before Anna had sat down, the carriage moved off.

Fanny's mouth dropped open.

'But, Anna!' she said, forgetting for a second that they weren't on speaking terms. 'What about everyone else? Where's Mr Terry?'

'Oh, he must come with my uncle and aunts,' Anna said. 'I really can't face another minute with him.'

For a moment, Fanny wasn't quite sure what to do with her face. It seemed to be passing through a whole number of expressions all by itself.

There was a pause.

Then, at the same instant, they both burst out laughing.

'Oh, Fanny,' Anna sighed as the convulsions subsided.

'He's just a bit … well … you know. In the library just now, he was *blowing his nose* so loudly.'

Fanny glowed inside. All at once they were back in accord, as if they'd never stopped being cousins who loved and understood each other. Spontaneously she reached out and took Anna's hand. Anna gripped it tight.

'Anna, you've got to do something about him,' Fanny said.

'Yes, I know,' Anna said, decisively, as if it were all absolutely agreed between them, and there was no need to argue or even to talk about it any more.

Fanny's feet practically soared up the steps to the gatehouse of Chilham Castle. Everything was going to be all right! Anna was going to break it off. And perhaps tonight she might find, *they both* might find, the perfect husband.

As soon as she and Anna stepped on to the draw-bridge, illuminated with blazing torches, Fanny knew that she was going to dance better than she'd ever danced before.

There were crowds of dancers flooding through the castle's grim gateway, ladies with late roses plaited into their hair, gentlemen in velvet coats, officers in their red jackets. The scent of the damp gardens down below in the old moat hung heavy in the air.

The ballroom was the ancient dark-panelled hall of the castle, and Fanny and Anna took their places at once for the country dance, standing side by side. And opposite them stood a couple of perfectly serviceable gentlemen to dance with! It had been easy! Fanny had got herself to this point with hardly a twinge of that horrible fear of being stranded partnerless.

It was Anna, of course, who'd beckoned to Lord Smedley and his friend as soon as they'd entered the ballroom, and the haughty lord had obediently followed her instructions. Now it was Lord Smedley who bowed down dutifully before Fanny. The wild lord! Tame at her command!

It was unprecedented. Fanny fleetingly remembered her fear and dismay at the first dance of the season. But now she could curtsy, and twirl her fan, and clap to the beat with abandon. Anna was happy; she was happy. Even Lord Smedley no longer seemed proud and distant and terrifying. Throughout their dance together he kept giving her little winks. Perhaps he was human after all.

At the end of the dance, she and Lord Smedley were panting and hot. They stood near the open door to the courtyard, and Fanny wafted her fan in his face for him. She felt that all the other young ladies in the room, and their mamas, must be looking at her, and wondering what she was saying.

But curiously, she didn't seem to mind.

'Do you remember,' she asked slyly, 'how you wouldn't dance with us, Anna and me, way back in the spring?'

He laughed, but had the grace to look uneasy.

'I do!' he said. 'That was before I knew you. I was rude,' he admitted, looking at his shoes, 'but it was because you and your cousin looked so *uncomfortable*. You looked like you'd be terrible partners, no conversation, just waiting to be dragged around like sacks of flour. And look at you now, Miss Austen! You are quite the accomplished flirt.'

Fanny smacked his arm with her fan, half pleased, half shocked.

'I apologise,' he said formally, placing his hand on his heart. '*You* are certainly not a flirt, although I refuse to rule out the possibility for your cousin. But really, Miss Austen, you are the prettiest young lady here tonight.'

Fanny found that her neck had somehow arched itself up like a swan's. She was pleased and proud, although she tried to look reproving.

She could tell, somehow, that Lord Smedley wasn't really flirting with her. He was teasing her, joking with her, almost like someone who might become a friend.

'I'll tell you what it is,' he said, even more confidentially. 'All the gentlemen know that you're taken. You and that parson Drummer have an understanding, haven't you? Makes you safe to dance with.'

'What in Heaven do you mean?'

Aghast, Fanny felt that her neck, swanlike a second ago, must now be stained with an ugly blush. She was mortified to learn that her and Mr Drummer's names had been linked. She had been too bold. She had taken things for granted.

'Oh no,' he said, seeing her dismay. 'Oh no, I don't mean to suggest anything improper. It's just that as a man you notice such a thing. Or, I mean to say ...'

He looked out into the courtyard as if in search of clarity, but found it not. He shrugged, and looked down at her through those eyelashes, thick as a girl's.

It was almost as if he was considering whether to take the risk of speaking honestly to her. That was, it seemed, against the rules of a ball.

'Or, I mean to say, a fellow can dance with you, without the fear of being forced by that mother of yours to offer you his hand!'

Six months ago, Fanny would have been confounded. But now she couldn't help but feel that he had paid her something of a compliment in speaking so freely. There

171

was truth in what he said. Yes, her mother – perhaps all the mamas – could be a bit ridiculous.

'Ah, but she does it out of love,' Fanny said, in a rush of fondness.

'As is only right,' he said gallantly, 'for she must be proud of her daughter. But will she let you marry that parson dog? That's the question. I haven't seen him about much, and he's not here tonight, is he? Where has he got to?'

Fanny turned away. She could not answer these questions, did not want to, did not feel that they should even have been asked.

She'd been feeling so sophisticated as she'd danced with the lord, but now the bottom seemed suddenly to have fallen out of the evening.

She mumbled something to Lord Smedley and stumbled away from him, trying to lose herself in the swirling crowd. Had she really made herself seem unobtainable, off the market? Did the neighbourhood really think that she was destined for the one man she could never marry?

Fanny sank down on to the bench for young ladies, pretending that she was tired and was just enjoying watching.

But her mind was busy.

Lord Smedley seemed to believe that it was at least

possible that she might marry Mr Drummer, that her parents *might conceivably* say yes. She must think that over carefully, because perhaps there would never be anyone else. Soon she was lost to the world, not at all embarrassed to be sitting and gazing into space instead of dancing. She had something much more delicious to think about instead.

Chapter 24

Aunt Jane's bedroom, Godmersham Park

The next morning, Fanny couldn't wait to find out what might happen next with Anna and Mr Terry. It would take her mind off her painful conversation with Lord Smedley, and the half-awful, half-delightful turmoil in her thoughts.

She and her cousin had come home so late they'd fallen asleep immediately, like baby Cassie did after bolting one of her milky meals. Yet Anna was already up and gone when Fanny opened her eyes. Where was she? Was she tackling Mr Terry? Or was she making it up with him again?

Fanny groaned and stretched and scratched her back under her nightgown, properly and satisfyingly.

But her own situation came creeping back into her mind. Her reputation was at risk! People had gossiped about her!

'Completely untrue!'

Fanny said the words out loud stoutly, almost as if practising saying them to her mother. 'There's nothing in what Lord Smedley said about me and Mr Drummer having an understanding. It's nonsense.'

Yet something deep in her bowels felt out of place. Almost as if she were lying to herself. They'd never spoken, but they'd … looked.

She put on her dressing gown and went to give her usual tap at Aunt Jane's door.

'Come in, Fanny,' Aunt Jane called from within. 'I warn you I'm still in bed.'

Aunt Jane had been dancing too, last night at the Chilham Ball. As Fanny entered, she lifted herself up on her elbows.

'Come on, my poor little waif,' Aunt Jane said, 'jump in.' She lifted the cover invitingly.

Fanny hurled herself across the room. It was true that her feet were cold.

She hadn't been in her aunt's bed since she was little. She tucked herself in and folded down the counterpane neatly over their two bodies. They lay there, side by side, like figures on a tomb in a church, looking up at fringes on the canopy over the bed's head. It occurred to Fanny that her aunt had quite a fancy bed for a spinster with no fortune.

'So, Fanny,' Aunt Jane said after a while. 'Tell me all your secrets.'

'Well, Anna says that she can't marry Mr Terry after all, because of his eyebrows.'

'His eyebrows!' Aunt Jane burst out laughing.

'Well, you know, his tufty eyebrows, and all the other annoying things too.'

'Good,' said Aunt Jane. 'So that's settled. Poor Anna, though, having to break it to him. Was that what you two were talking about last night? I saw all that winking and whispering. You're as thick as thieves again, aren't you? And what did the fascinating young lord have to say? You came away looking all pink. You want to watch out with him, you know. He's dangerous.'

'Well,' Fanny began, uncertain how much to tell. Then she decided that there was no point in holding anything back. It would be such a relief to talk about Mr Drummer.

All her confusion seemed suddenly to drain away, and she felt much refreshed, lying peacefully there in bed with her aunt. The sun was coming up outside, she saw, the golden sun of September. She tried to think how to begin.

'Aunt Jane,' she said. 'I really, really like Dominic Drummer. And I think that he likes me.'

'Fanny!' said Aunt Jane. 'Tell me at once. Are you in love?'

Fanny couldn't answer. 'I'm not sure,' she said. 'What does it feel like?'

'Does it *hurt*?' said Aunt Jane. 'Can you think of nothing else in the whole world apart from him? Take your time, now. You might confuse love with infatuation, just at first. They feel similar.'

'Well, perhaps it hurts a little,' Fanny conceded. 'But also I'm worried about what people might say, and then there's the mess he's in, you know, and I want to help him. But it's all so difficult, knowing how to.'

'Ah,' said Aunt Jane. 'He *is* difficult to help. Such a proud young man. The penniless often are, you know, proud I mean. I am very proud myself.'

'If he only he were rich!' Fanny groaned. 'Then it would be easy!'

'Being rich comes with problems too, Fanny,' said

Aunt Jane. 'I think it's nicest to be comfortably in-between.'

'Aunt Jane,' Fanny began, taking advantage of the fact that they were in such a good situation for sharing secrets. 'I know … that … well, I know you're penniless, or something like. But I also know someone has paid for Mr Drummer to have better lodgings, and has been helping him with money. I think that … might … have been you?'

She did not dare turn her head on the pillow to look over at her aunt.

There was a big sigh.

'Yes, I have been able to help him. I do have money,' Aunt Jane admitted, 'though not as much as your father and mother. It's money I have earned myself, and I'm very proud of that.'

Now Fanny glanced across. Aunt Jane's knife-like nose was pointing straight at the ceiling, as if she didn't want to be asked any questions.

Of course Fanny felt desperate to ask how on earth Aunt Jane had earned this money. Earning money, her mother constantly told her, was the least ladylike thing she could possibly do.

That must be why Aunt Jane kept it so secret, because she lived here at Godmersham Park as Elizabeth's guest.

Had Fanny's aunt done it through sewing and embroidering? She was very skilled at such things, and made the most wonderful presents with her needle.

But Aunt Jane's nose invited no questions, and Fanny decided not to address the issue. To talk about it would implicitly criticise her own mother.

'So … if you helped him,' she said slowly, feeling her way on to safer ground, 'do you also think that Mr Drummer must be innocent? Could we perhaps … go to see him again?'

'I think he *is* innocent,' said Aunt Jane, 'and that's why I took you to the House of Correction, so you can see that sometimes innocent people end up there. For all Anna's talk of justice and right and wrong, it's money that speaks in this world.'

She sighed, and rolled her head so she was looking into Fanny's face. 'But there's one thing, Fanny,' she said very seriously. 'If we go to see him, and if you eventually decide you *don't* like him, you could lose your reputation. You've got to keep it safe if you're to make the sort of marriage that your parents want for you.'

At that Aunt Jane gave Fanny a very sharp stare.

Fanny realised that her aunt hadn't said 'the marriage that *you* want'. There was a whirring sensation in her head. What did she want – for herself?

'I promise,' she said quickly, avoiding the unspoken question.

'Now, I'll tell you what's going to happen about your Mr Drummer,' her aunt said, propping herself up and reaching for her spectacles. 'I've been reading in the newspapers about similar cases, and I have written to Mr Sprack the thief-taker for advice. We'll go into Canterbury today, to meet him, and to see what he thinks. He is coming down on this morning's stagecoach from London.'

Fanny gulped. Her aunt was in correspondence with the most famous thief-taker in London! Everyone had heard of the ingenious Mr Sprack!

'How did you know where to write?' she asked at once. 'I really can't imagine my father doing that.'

'Oh, I met him once, in London,' Aunt Jane said vaguely. 'At a party.' She was now unfolding and rereading a letter. 'Yes, the meeting is at the Star,' she said. 'At midday.'

'Huh,' Fanny said.

She didn't know quite what else to add. Aunt Jane going to parties in London! And knowing exciting people like thief-takers! It was almost as if she wasn't quite the dry old stick George insisted that she was.

'Better get dressed,' Aunt Jane was saying. 'Our business can't wait.' She swung herself bolt upright. In her long white nightgown, her thin figure looked like a corpse in its shroud arisen from its grave.

Fanny slipped out of the bed too, excited but nervous. To meet a real-life thief-taker! The very thought filled her with trepidation. Would he be greasy and dishonest, like the warder at the House of Correction?

But at least Aunt Jane would be there.

And a secret part of her was delighted that Aunt Jane had chosen Fanny herself for this work. Not Anna, but Fanny alone.

Chapter 25

The Star Inn, Canterbury

With practised smoothness – or so it now seemed to Fanny – Aunt Jane had talked her way into getting the carriage.

'The children's clothes,' she'd explained, 'and a few small errands of my own. Fanny and I can bring back that package of tea you wanted, Elizabeth, the one from London. It should arrive at the Star Inn on the midday stage, don't you think?'

'Certainly, certainly,' Fanny's father had said. 'Enjoy yourselves. I can't think how you have the energy after such a late night.'

Fanny now climbed into the carriage with an unusually straight spine. She could imagine the eyes of her brothers and sisters boring into her from their nursery window, wondering where she was off to.

She imagined them saying, 'Look, Fanny's going somewhere secret with Aunt Jane. Yet she's always telling us that God will punish us if we deceive.'

But Aunt Jane hadn't lied: she and Fanny truly were going to the Star Inn.

When they got there, Fanny headed for the staircase which led to the big dancing room.

'Oh no,' said Aunt Jane, 'we're not going up there. This way, Fanny, into the bar.'

Fanny had never been into such a smoke-stained, sticky, dark and noisy interior. Each seat was taken by a farmer with a foaming tankard who was engaged in shouting at his friends. Behind the bar a woman with hefty forearms was chopping ham, as vigorously as if she were chopping off the heads of her enemies.

There was a slight but noticeable dip in the volume as Aunt Jane and Fanny entered.

Fanny wished that she wasn't dressed in such bright white muslin, and that her bonnet did not have such obviously expensive silk flowers on it. She caught the barmaid looking at her as if she were out of place.

Aunt Jane just gave a loud sniff, and forged forward into the crowd.

Near the window stood a particularly tall-backed bench, and on a bright day like this, the dazzle outside made anyone sitting upon it dark and shadowy to the eye.

But there *was* someone there. He wore a tall hat, and although she could only see his silhouette, Fanny could tell that there was a long cloak thrown back from his shoulders. Against the bench lay a staff. On the table before the man stood not a tankard of ale but a little conical goblet, and a bottle.

'Jane Austen,' he grunted, as Fanny's aunt stood before him. 'Good Lord, it's Jane Austen, as I live and breathe. Fire and brimstone, the very lady. The battleaxe herself.'

He took off his hat and placed it over his breast, and stared at Fanny's aunt as if in awe.

To her surprise, he was teasing Aunt Jane.

Fanny raised her eyebrows. People often sighed, or turned away, at her aunt's somewhat intimidating approach. They did not stare at her in mock enraptured attention.

Aunt Jane never minced or smirked, but there was something about the set of her head that told Fanny she was pleased.

'Sit down,' he said, 'and do me the honour of taking a

184

drink with me.' He fished another little glass out of the darkness at his feet, and poured Aunt Jane a rich golden cordial of some kind. He glanced at Fanny herself.

'Too young,' said Aunt Jane, seating herself on a stool and gesturing Fanny to take the place next to the thief-taker.

Fanny peered sideways, timidly, at his seamed skin, his silvery beard, his eyes that were buried deep in his face. His half-submerged eyeballs nevertheless had a bright glint to them, and his gaze swivelled across the taproom and back with intensity. She had the sense that if she'd suddenly blindfolded him, he could still have described everyone within the inn.

'Light favours us,' he said to Fanny. She was embarrassed that he'd noticed her scrutiny, but didn't know what he meant.

'They can only see the outline of the bench against the window,' he explained. 'And we've got both exits covered.'

Fanny now noticed that there was another little door opposite, leading directly out to the stable yard.

Fanny saw that Aunt Jane was giving her rare thin smile. She downed her cordial in one.

'Now, Mr Sprack,' she said in her abrupt way. 'I don't want to keep you from your work on the trail of those evil slave traders. I've been following your progress in the *Times of London*. Most impressive. I'm glad the matter brought you into Kent.'

He gave a grave and courteous nod to acknowledge her compliment.

It made Fanny think that he must respect her aunt's opinion a good deal.

'Anyway, here's what's happened in Canterbury,' Aunt Jane was saying. 'I think I can detect in it echoes of the recent trickery in Bath that I read about in the *Gazette*.'

She outlined events so far, explaining that Mr Drummer had gone to buy gloves yet had inexplicably found himself in possession of stolen lace. She stressed that to the best of her knowledge Mr Drummer was a straightforward, honourable young man.

'Quite an ordinary young man,' Aunt Jane said, 'but definitely honourable.'

Fanny looked down at her fingers. What did Aunt Jane really think of Mr Drummer? Did she think that he was someone Fanny should marry? Fanny realised now that her aunt had somehow managed to keep her views very much to herself.

Mr Sprack picked up his staff and planted it on the floor between his knees, clasping it in both hands. He leaned forward, and cleared his throat.

186

Both Fanny and Aunt Jane leaned forward too. They didn't want to miss a word, nor for Mr Sprack to have to speak so loudly that others might hear.

The din of the farmers had returned to normal, and no one appeared to be paying them any attention. Yet Mr Sprack did not immediately address the case.

'This one here,' he said in his breathy, whispering voice, cocking his head at Fanny. 'I could use her. She'll pass for quality, which is hard to find in my business. I can use her as bait, for messages, trick-work. Train her up, I would, Miss Austen. Does she need a bob or two?'

Aunt Jane laughed. The suggestion obviously pleased her.

'No, no,' she said. 'Miss Fanny is quite the clever girl, certainly worthy of your training, but her parents have other plans for her. Not to speak of any plans she may have for herself. Although, Mr Sprack,' Aunt Jane added, as if she felt she ought to, 'my niece *is* quality, you know. She won't just *pass* for quality, she *is* the real thing.'

'Worth more than rubies,' Mr Sprack continued. Fanny looked at him again, and one of his black, currant-like eyes winked at her. All of a sudden, she felt comfortable with him and his stealthy ways. She could imagine him passing along the dark streets of a city like London as if he were a ghost, seeing, but not being seen.

'So, Mr Sprack? Your verdict on the case?'

He sighed and went on, as if unaware of the tumult he'd awakened in Fanny. How exciting to be the assistant of such a man! What sights she might see, what adventures she might have! But then, how adamantly her mother would refuse to let her.

How shocked her mother would be, even just to see her here in the common barroom of the Star.

Now Mr Sprack spoke, and with confidence. 'It's a new trick that crooked shopkeepers have started playing just recently,' he said. 'They use it on customers who seem a bit dreamy, or not very wise about the world. People like your Mr Drummer. Was it known in the town that he had rich friends?'

'Yes,' said Aunt Jane. 'It was known that he'd come here as parson to my brother Edward on his estate just outside town. Edward is one of the big men of the neighbourhood.'

'The shopkeeper waits till a dreamy-looking customer buys something – and he *did* buy a pair of gloves, you said, Miss Austen? And then, while doing up the parcel, the shopkeeper *slips in something else*. Like this lace, in your case. The customer leaves, the shopkeeper "realises" that something's gone missing, accosts the customer and hey-ho – the evidence is right there in his hands! Or her hands. Women have been victims of this trick too.'

'But why would the shopkeeper want Mr Drummer to go to prison, or even be transported?' Fanny asked.

'Ah,' said Aunt Jane, digging about in her little bag and drawing out a small piece of newsprint. 'This is from the *Bath Gazette*, it's the case I mentioned, Mr Sprack. It sounds similar. The idea, you see, is *extortion*.'

'That's right,' confirmed Mr Sprack. 'The shopkeeper then says, to the victim, or ideally to the victim's rich friends, "If you pay me a hundred pounds, or thereabouts, I will retract my testimony to the magistrate. And then you, Mr Customer, you will avoid the risk of being tried and perhaps being transported to the criminal colonies." It's devilish, isn't it? Would you want to run the risk of going to court, of having an overloaded magistrate making a hasty judgement upon you, if you could be sure of getting off? You never know which way things will fall in the courtroom.'

Aunt Jane was nodding, as if in recognition.

'That's about the size of it,' Mr Sprack concluded. 'For rich folk, one hundred or even two hundred pounds is worth it. The risk of the prison ships and a life in the hellhole of Australia is not worth taking.'

Fanny wrinkled her brows.

'But why would they send Mr Drummer to the hell-hole of *Australia*?' she asked. 'It's an awfully long way.'

'Because the lace was very valuable, Fanny,' Aunt Jane explained. 'It was worth, oh, thirty or forty shillings. And if you get convicted of a theft like that, then to the colonies you go.'

'But magistrates are there to make sure that such mistakes don't happen!' Fanny cried.

'And how much time,' her aunt replied crisply, 'have you seen my brother Edward putting into his duties as a magistrate? How carefully does he investigate each case?'

Fanny hung her head, reluctant to admit the answer. But she knew it was 'not very much'. Her father was just so busy, so sociable, so wrapped up in his hounds and his friends, his lands and his debts.

'Yet there's something a bit odd here,' said Mr Sprack. 'In the other cases I've seen, the criminals made contact with the accused, or at least with the accused's rich friends. They had to make it clear that they *could* be bought off. And you said that Mr Drummer hasn't mentioned such an approach? He's just been left to rot in prison with no word from anyone?'

'I've thought of that,' said Aunt Jane. 'I think the

wicked shopkeeper didn't realise how proud Mr Drummer would be, and how reluctant to ask for help, and how busy and perhaps lazy my brother might be, therefore failing to offer it.'

'But that's so unfair!' Fanny cried. 'It's awful! Mr Drummer could be sent away on a prison ship, and he *hasn't* stolen that lace, has he? How can we prove the shopkeeper *is* crooked?'

'Well, I think there might be a way,' Aunt Jane said. 'The date of poor Mr Drummer's trial is fast approaching, and I think the crooked shopkeeper will be getting ready to approach his rich friends at Godmersham, to see if they will take the trouble to buy him out of trouble. I propose that we – you and I, Fanny – draw this to a head. See if we can make it happen.'

Fanny shrank back against the hard boards of the bench. Her aunt was talking in a frightening way. Mr Sprack was looking at her too, and nodding.

'Um, shouldn't we just … tell my father?' she asked quietly.

'No, Fanny,' Aunt Jane said firmly. 'For several reasons. Firstly, he's got so much on his mind, and he's so inefficient about his business. And Elizabeth with child again, and quite ill with it too.'

Fanny, to her shame, realised that yes, her mother had

been looking very heavy and tired. And she, Fanny, had not really asked, or helped, or done anything about it. She'd been afraid her mother might snap at her.

Fanny nodded.

'And,' her aunt continued, 'it's a delicate matter. I invited Mr Drummer to live at Godmersham. It's my fault, in a way. I want to try to get him out of gaol.'

'If I were you,' said Mr Sprack, stroking his beard, 'I would send this one –' he gestured at Fanny – 'into the shop, to ask a few questions. See if anyone is eager to meet a well-dressed friend of your Mr Drummer's. Someone with a shilling or two to spare.'

So she was to bait the trap! She was to see if she could tempt a potential blackmailer into providing evidence of his or her treachery. They were talking almost as if Fanny were a thief-taker herself.

'I think you will play the part very well, Fanny,' Aunt Jane added, 'because you always look so demure.'

Despite the backhanded nature of the compliment, Fanny sat up a little. Mr Sprack had said that her manner was a valuable quality in a thief-taker.

'And good luck to you,' said Mr Sprack.

At that moment, there was the ear-splitting sound of the horn being blown, and a stir in the bar.

'I've got to get that coach,' he said. 'I'll have to be

leaving you. I'm after my slavers, you know, and I think they're making for the ships at Deptford. Write to tell me how it goes, Miss Austen.'

With that he rose – he really was quite astonishingly tall – drew his cloak around him and slipped out of the little door into the yard. It was almost as if he'd never been there at all.

And Fanny and Aunt Jane were shockingly and quite inappropriately left alone in the common bar of the Star Inn, with two used glasses and what Fanny feared might be an empty bottle of brandy.

Chapter 26

The draper's shop, Canterbury

Fanny was more nervous than she'd been in her whole life as she strolled down the last bit of pavement towards the draper's shop where Mr Drummer had come a cropper.

Or to be more accurate, a 'stroll' was what she was aiming at. She felt that she must be walking so self-consciously that everyone in the street would be wondering what was wrong with her.

Aunt Jane was waiting in the carriage so that Fanny could – as her aunt put it – maintain her 'cloak of anonymity' as she went on her mission.

'Or shall I come with you?' Aunt Jane had asked, at the very last minute. Perhaps she'd noticed the way that Fanny kept nervously picking at the skin of her thumb.

'No, thank you,' said Fanny. She could tell that for some reason Aunt Jane really wanted her to face this task alone.

Hey-ho, Fanny thought to herself, *perhaps this will train me for a life as an assistant thief-taker. Someone like that really could be the heroine of a story.*

And yet even on ordinary days she disliked going into shops, and asking for what she wanted, and being made to feel that she was wasting the shopkeeper's time if after all she did not buy what was offered. She much preferred going in with her mother, who would sweep in and buy or not buy and think nothing of it.

Fanny hesitated on the step of the shop, desperately longing to go skipping back to James and the carriage and Aunt Jane as fast as her feet could carry her.

She pretended to look through the bow window at the wares displayed behind it. Swathes of silk and cotton spilt down from hooks, enticing her with their glowing sheen.

It was no good. She *must* go in. She clutched the shopping list in her hand, making the paper crackle, and banged the door open.

Inside it was dark and close, and the shop seemed to

have retained something of the summer's stuffy heat. Fanny loosened the ties of her bonnet and pushed it back on her head. Its sides had prevented her from looking round the room. She wanted to scan the place for suspicious signs, just as Mr Sprack might do himself.

This was a different draper to the one the Godmersham family usually patronised. But it all looked familiar: babies' caps, and stockings for gentlemen, and dress material, and India muslins all stacked in a profusion of wooden shelves and cubbyholes.

The counter was worn smooth, perhaps from the rolling out of so many bales of cambric over the years, Fanny thought. And there, prominently displayed upon it, was a card saying, *Gloves for gentlemen. Five shillings. Excellent price.*

Her heart nearly skipped a beat. Yes, surely these were the very same gloves which – to the penniless Mr Drummer – had seemed such a good bargain. Until the transaction had landed him in prison.

She approached the counter and saw, with a start, that in the dark corner behind it stood a stocky, aggressive-looking woman. She was staring at Fanny in a way that suggested she'd been watching her ever since she'd entered the shop.

Two other ladies were examining silk thread over by the window, and Fanny's courage wavered at the thought of doing her business before witnesses.

But she approached the counter, and said good afternoon. The saleswoman's pugnacious face was rather like those of the fighting dogs her brother George adored.

The woman was dressed in a sprigged muslin gown in a pink that clashed unpleasantly with the red of her face. She was obviously supposed to be wearing a delightful gown that might tempt the customers to buy something similar, but Fanny thought that it was so tight for her, and so unbecomingly frilled, that she looked rather like a dressed-up pig.

She also had an unexpectedly low and gruff voice.

'Yes, miss?'

The words were deferential, but the tone was not.

But this at least was a prompt for Fanny to begin.

'I would like,' she said, consulting her list, 'a new chemise for a four-year-old.' Louie's had worn out. The woman rooted about, as if it were a great imposition, and found an article which Fanny had, regretfully, to pronounce too small. Louie was growing so fast. Eventually another one was settled upon.

'Have you a ready-made shirt for a boy of nine?'

197

'Have you fine folk so much money you buy such things?' the woman asked scornfully. 'What about sewing it for yourself?'

Fanny privately thought that the shop would go bust if the woman was so reluctant to make sales.

'My mother is so busy,' she explained, although she really felt it was no business of anyone else's.

But the loud silence behind her from the bow window told her that the two matrons were likewise judging the family which bought rather than made its children's clothes.

Fanny coughed before she felt able to continue.

'Five handkerchiefs.'

'Five!'

'My father loses them so often,' Fanny felt compelled to add.

'Well, this is going to cost a pretty penny,' the woman said, beginning to pack up Fanny's purchases.

'But you can send the bill, can't you?' Fanny asked. 'To Godmersham Park?'

The words had an electrifying effect. The woman's hands stopped work immediately, and she was looking harder than ever at Fanny.

'Would you like,' she said in a tough, low hiss, 'to buy anything else?'

'No, thank you,' said Fanny, leaning back as far as she could without actually moving her feet and therefore looking as if she were in retreat.

'Not even ...' The woman leaned closer, and Fanny thought she could detect a taint on her breath. Her face looked oily in the warm room. '... a piece of lace?'

The shopkeeper began to thrum her fingernails on the wood of the counter. Fanny noticed, on her left thumb, the nasty-looking stain of a wart. And then, as if by magic, among the handkerchiefs, there was indeed a piece of lace.

She looked at it, aghast, then up again at the woman. Not a flicker on the woman's face. What did she mean? Was this a signal?

It must be!

And yet behind her, the two other customers had carried on talking as normal, just as if nothing were out of the ordinary.

Fanny looked down at the counter again.

'And the price?' she asked.

The answer came in a whisper, but immediately and confidently. 'Two hundred pounds.'

Fanny almost leaped out of her skin. It was happening! Yes, just as Aunt Jane thought, she had set in motion the next stage of the plot in which Mr Drummer had been caught.

'It's not a lot of money for the Godmersham family,' the woman said aggressively, answering Fanny's gesture of surprise rather than the words she'd been too shocked to speak.

Fanny looked at her hands, unsure how to respond.

Aunt Jane had told her that when the moment came, she'd know what to do.

She thought hard.

'I haven't such money with me,' she said. 'It'll take me time to get it. But how may such a piece of lace be purchased?'

'Why, right here, at the shop,' the woman replied, holding Fanny's eyes. Fanny felt like a mouse, trapped in the gaze of a predatory cat. Her knees were almost knocking together under the strain of standing there. This was extortion! It was against the law!

And yet, Fanny realised, the woman had said nothing compromising. Indeed, the two women now turning to the rolls of ribbon in the corner had heard every word.

'No,' Fanny said, gathering her courage. 'I cannot come here with it. My parents would not approve, and it will be hard for me to gather such a sum. But I could perhaps find it, and give it to … a messenger. At night, probably, would be best. Perhaps …'

Fanny thought very hard.

'Perhaps at the little temple on the hill in Godmersham Park. That way I could slip out and not be missed.'

The woman snorted.

'Fine notions of behaviour among the young ladies these days!' she said. 'Creeping out at night, helping their gentleman friends.'

Fanny felt suddenly hot with rage. What business of this woman's? Helping Mr Drummer was the right thing to do! Otherwise he might be sent to Australia! And then she remembered the crinkles at the corners of his eyes as he smiled. Yes, helping Dominic Drummer was not only the right thing to do, it was also a pleasant thing to do.

The thought gave her courage. Fanny felt a severe expression settle over her face, and she lifted her chin and simply ignored the woman's comment. It wasn't worth dignifying with a response.

The shopkeeper interpreted Fanny's silence as assent, and now she gave a curt nod. 'Tonight, if you please,' she added, picking up a pencil to tot up Fanny's purchases. Then she began to wrap them in paper. Fanny watched very hard to make sure that the lace did not make its way into the parcels, but it had once again disappeared from the countertop.

All was done at last, and the woman nodded at her once more, not in a friendly way, but in complicity.

'All right,' Fanny said over her shoulder, as she began to leave the shop. 'Tonight!'

Chapter 27

The attics, Godmersham Park

A unt Jane greeted Fanny with a big smile.

'You did it, didn't you?' she said at once. 'You negotiated the fee to buy the shopkeeper off, and set up the handover rendezvous as well.'

'How did you know?' cried Fanny, a little disappointed that she hadn't been able to keep her aunt in pleasurable anticipation, as she'd hoped. She'd imagined them driving along in the carriage, and Aunt Jane begging her to tell her what had happened. Fanny would have sighed, and told the story only after being soothed and indulged. But her aunt had guessed straight away.

'By your walk,' Aunt Jane confessed. 'You came

bouncing down the street as if it were your birthday. Unlike when you went *to* the shop, as if walking to the gallows. So Mr Drummer is a step nearer to freedom!'

Mr Drummer. Mr Drummer. There was no time, however, for thinking about him now, because her aunt was busy asking her about every detail of what had happened inside the shop. When Fanny reported how the piece of white lace had mysteriously 'appeared' on the counter, Aunt Jane clapped her hands in delight.

'A prestidigitarian!' she said.

'What's that?' asked Fanny.

'Someone with very quick fingers, someone who could work as a professional pickpocket, for example,' her aunt explained. 'I'll warrant that that draper's shop doesn't make its money as a draper's, but is just a front for a den of thieves. It's the exact same trick I read about in the newspaper from Bath. And now we have them on the back foot! Well done, Fanny!'

Fanny glowed. To her surprise, the journey had passed so quickly that they were already in the park.

Fanny Austen, thief-taker, sang a voice in her head. She could have hugged herself. Until she remembered that the next stage of the challenge would unfold tonight, out at the temple in the dark. It wasn't so much fun to consider that.

Fanny prepared herself to behave in front of her family as if exactly nothing had happened. As if she and Aunt Jane had never even thought of going on a mission, undertaken with a thief-taker's advice, for the entrapment of an extortionist.

But just as the carriage entered the last bend of the drive, it gave a violent swerve.

'What can James be thinking of?' Aunt Jane exclaimed.

Fanny snatched off her bonnet and poked her head out of the window. She saw that a farm wagon, travelling at great speed, had almost forced their carriage off the road. James drew the horses to a halt.

'He almost put us in the ditch!' he called out. 'Are you ladies hurt?'

Clouds of dust still lingered in the air.

Fanny and Aunt Jane, sobered by the shock, decided to get down and walk across the grass to the door.

Fanny hoped that the house would be quiet. She wanted to be by herself, to think about how Mr Drummer might thank her for what she'd done, dipping down his chin to disguise a bashful smile …

But as soon as she opened the door of the hall, she discovered all her siblings gathered there, and a great deal of confusion.

'Fanny!' cried her mother. 'You're back. Where have you been?'

Fanny tried to think of an appropriate answer.

'Meeting with a notorious thief-taker' wouldn't do it.

But her mother, as usual, wasn't really listening.

'Now, Fan,' her mother was saying, urgently. 'You must go at once and find Anna. She's very upset.'

'But what has happened?' Fanny asked. 'Is someone hurt? What is it?'

She'd already lost her mother's attention. Elizabeth was picking up a weeping Louie and patting her on the back.

Lizzie was at Fanny's elbow.

'Did you see the farm cart?'

'See it?' cried Fanny. 'It nearly killed Aunt Jane and me!'

'That was Mr Terry,' said Lizzie. 'Anna gave him his marching orders. She was terribly upset. He insisted on leaving at once, and the cart was the only thing to hand, seeing as how the carriage had mysteriously disappeared. Why did you and Aunt Jane take so long at the shops?' she asked with interest. 'Did something happen?'

'Never mind that now,' said Fanny, taking advantage of the situation. 'Where is Anna?'

Lizzie said she'd last been seen storming off upstairs.

'I'll find her,' Fanny promised. 'I'll do my best to calm her down.'

She picked up her skirts and ran upstairs. To her own room. No, it was empty. To Aunt Jane's room. Empty again. Aunt Jane was presumably still downstairs, enjoying the uproar in the hall. Fanny was about to go down again and try the library when she remembered a wet afternoon she and Anna had once spent in the attics, running up and down the rough-boarded corridor and draping themselves with old curtains in one of the storerooms.

She galloped up the rickety flight that led right up into the garrets and roofs of the house.

'Anna?'

Everything was still. A bumblebee buzzed its slow way between the banisters at the top of the stairs, and a shaft of September sun made the motes of dust spin and jig.

It was so silent that Fanny nearly went back down to look for Anna elsewhere.

But she noticed a scuff mark in the dust on the boards at the top of the stairs.

She crept along the passage through the attics. Which door led to the room with the curtains and old cushions and mouldering swags of velvet? *This one*, she thought. She pushed it, and it opened with a ghastly creak.

Yes! There was Anna. She was lying face down, upon a rolled-up carpet, and her shoulders were heaving.

Fanny sprang forward and placed her hand on her cousin's back.

'Oh, Anna, don't cry, don't cry,' she said. 'You were brave, like a heroine. You did the right thing! You couldn't marry him, it was all wrong.'

'Oh, Fanny,' Anna said in a choked voice. 'He looked so sad, like a hurt dog.'

'He wasn't right for you,' said Fanny fiercely. 'He wasn't half as nice as Mr Drummer, for example.' She suddenly thought that maybe Anna would feel better if she had something else to think about. 'You know Mr Drummer?' Fanny said with satisfaction. 'Anna, I've got something to tell you about Mr Drummer!'

Anna went silent, and tense. She rolled away from Fanny and sat up bolt upright, looking out through the little dormer window.

'Oh,' she said. 'So, now you're going to marry Mr Drummer, are you? And live in the Godmersham parsonage, where I was supposed to live! You win again, Fanny.'

The unfairness of the accusation hit Fanny with all the force of a speeding farm cart.

'Anna!' she managed to say. 'That's ridiculous!'

She sucked in her breath to start explaining why, but it was too late. Like a flash, Anna had leaped up and was shaking her fist, yes, actually shaking her fist in Fanny's face.

'Who are you, *Fanny Austen*,' Anna was saying, 'to tell me what to do? First you tell me to marry Mr Terry – yes, you did, you did tell me I had to marry him because no one else would marry me. An awful man like him! Then when I got engaged, you changed your mind, didn't you? You didn't like it, and you didn't like the thought of me living in your parsonage, and you made me break it off! And now I've got … I've got to go back home …'

Anna was coughing and crying so hard that she had to break off speaking to choke in some breath. But Fanny couldn't get a word in.

'And all the time,' Anna was ranting, 'you, *Fanny Austen*, are too scared and too rich to find someone for yourself, aren't you? And it's "Mr Drummer this and Mr Drummer that" because he's the safe option. Your parents will buy him for you, if you really want him, Fanny, won't they? Like a new horse or a new dog. You know nothing,' Anna concluded. 'You know nothing of what life is like if you don't have money. You've got too much money. It's made you stupid. You and I, we're not sisters, or cousins, or even friends. I hate you!'

Before Fanny could even answer, Anna had run out of the room. Fanny could hear her feet stomping along the dusty corridor. She was obviously determined that she should get away, and that Fanny should not follow.

Fanny collapsed, slowly, into a sitting position on the roll of carpet. Her heart bled for Anna's pain.

It's not my fault, she said to herself savagely. *Anna's just very sad that she had to hurt Mr Terry. So she wants to hurt other people.*

Fanny said this to herself several times, as if repeating it would make it true.

It was true.

But then she slumped forward, and shoved the heels of her hands into her eye sockets, and stared at the stars that wheeled there in the blackness.

It was true, yes, it was true that she was not responsible for Anna's grief.

Yet a tiny little truth worm uncoiled itself somewhere deep within Fanny's gut.

It was true that she *had* hated the thought of Anna living in the parsonage with Mr Terry.

It was true that she'd much preferred to imagine a life where Mr Drummer was set free and able to live in his own house once again.

And most of all, she'd spent a lot of time imagining a life in which her father and mother would come around to the idea that another person should join Mr Drummer in Godmersham parsonage.

That person being Fanny herself.

Chapter 28

Aunt Jane's bedroom, Godmersham Park

Anna's thundering footsteps had completely disappeared, and silence had long returned to the sunny attic, before Fanny felt able to move.

She slowly got to her feet, testing them to check if they were still working. Anna's horrible words had cut her deeply.

No longer cousins. No longer even friends.

There was only one thing to do. There was only one person who might be able to help her feel better.

She set off for Aunt Jane's room.

'Let her go,' Aunt Jane said, taking one look at Fanny's face. 'You've done your best, Fanny. You are not your cousin's keeper. She's feeling her way, you know. Part of that is exploring where you begin and where she ends. You know it's harder for her because she hasn't got a mother.'

Fanny had to share her own mother with nine other people. But she did remember that warm feeling when her mama combed a nasty knot out of her hair, or said what a serious little thing she was, and quite the cleverest of the family.

So Aunt Jane's words were cooling, like the mint balm she sometimes put on her skin. They allowed Fanny to crumble at last completely.

'Oh,' she sobbed, throwing herself into her aunt's arms, 'Anna said such horrible things.'

'Careful, careful, mind my pen,' said Aunt Jane, reaching round Fanny's shoulders to put it back on her desk. 'Look! I've ever so nearly got ink on your gown, and that would never do, would it? Not for Miss Goody-Goody, Smart-As-Paint, Tidy-Boots Fanny Austen?'

Fanny let out a hiccup.

All the time she was speaking, Aunt Jane was also giving Fanny the tightest of hugs. It was always the same with Aunt Jane; she never said exactly what you expected her to. But her teasing made Fanny feel a tiny bit better.

'Let Anna go,' said Aunt Jane again, as Fanny's gulps subsided and she regained control of her breathing.

'It's just so unfair,' Fanny said. 'I didn't ask to be born … rich. I don't even want to *be* rich if it makes other people despise me. And we don't *feel* rich here, you know that, even if Anna doesn't. My father says that there are so many expenses, and my mother constantly says that we're going short of the things we should have.'

'Never say that,' Aunt Jane said gravely, shunting Fanny over to the sofa. 'You are very comfortably off, here at Godmersham Park. Even if your father doesn't think so, you've got enough money to take the pressure off when it comes to marriage. Or indeed, choosing not to marry. Poor Anna, she feels so pushed and pulled.'

'But doesn't she have … *freedom*?' Fanny asked. 'My father and my mother would never have agreed, for example, if I'd wanted to marry Mr Terry. They'd have said it was undignified.'

For a tiny, treacherous second, she wondered if it was true, as Anna had said, that they *would* let her marry Mr Drummer if she really, really insisted. Could that ever really happen?

'Money,' said Jane, 'means choice. Not a lot of choice, girls don't get that. But it means a bit more choice.'

Fanny was struck by something in her aunt's voice.

214

'Aunt Jane, what about you?' she asked. 'You've never got married. And you haven't got all that much money to live on either.'

Aunt Jane looked at Fanny very hard.

'You think I haven't much money, hey, Fanny?'

Fanny blushed, and dropped her gaze.

'Well,' she stammered, 'from what my father and mother may have said …'

Aunt Jane gave a grim little laugh.

'You're right,' she said. 'My own father, your grandfather, was just as hard up as Anna's father is now. My brother Edward was the lucky one, getting adopted by the rich old lady who gave him this house, and marrying Elizabeth, who was rich herself. But I told you, I've plenty of money of my own. Even without a husband I could easily lay hands on the two hundred pounds our blackmailer thinks you're going to bring along to the temple this evening.'

Fanny felt her eyes bulging.

'But how did you earn so much money?' she asked. 'Two hundred pounds! That's a huge amount!' 'Money' was such a cold, dirty word. She felt reluctant, unladylike, even saying it. But Aunt Jane for once seemed in a mood to be clear about things formerly kept obscure.

'Can you keep a secret?' Aunt Jane whispered, holding

215

Fanny in her gaze almost like a snake. 'Can you keep the deepest, darkest secret I could tell you?'

Fanny nodded, silently, transfixed. She was almost in awe of her aunt, who seemed to know so much.

'I earned it,' Aunt Jane continued, speaking very softly, 'by writing novels. I got two hundred pounds for my last one. And there –' she flicked her eyes to the little writing desk – 'is the next.'

'Oh, nonsense,' Fanny cried. 'You're teasing me. You're, well, you're our aunt, not a famous novelist like, oh, I don't know, Fanny Burney.'

In reply, her aunt stood up, and went over to the shelves by the bed, and pulled out a couple of little volumes. She handed them to Fanny, who opened the title page. 'By a Lady' was all it said.

Aunt Jane smiled.

'But I've read this!' Fanny said. 'It was ever so funny. Everyone's read it, my mother and all of us!'

Aunt Jane was nodding.

'And did you really … write it? In secret?'

Aunt Jane was still nodding.

She watched and waited while Fanny processed the information.

Fanny's mouth slowly fell open. It all began to make sense! Those endless letters that her aunt wrote! They weren't letters … but works of fiction? And that's why her aunt cared so much about them, and hated to be disturbed?

'Fanny,' her aunt said at last, reaching out her hand to take back the books. 'You see that I have a secret, and that I've trusted you not to reveal it. My brother would not like it to be known that his sister was a dirty scribbler, earning money from her pen. But I *do* make money, lots of lovely money, and I like having my secret life that's a bit apart from the family and the rest of you.'

Thoughts were churning in Fanny's head.

'Aunt Jane, so is that why you never got married? Because you didn't need to?'

'Oh, that's a long story,' her aunt said. 'But you mustn't feel, and Anna mustn't feel, that it will be truly awful if you don't find a husband. It's simply not a vital thing to do at all. You're beginning to see that for yourself, aren't you? You're a clever enough girl. And as well as keeping my secret, you must be sure, *be quite sure*, of what you want, before you make any decisions about your Dominic Drummer. And now, if you've finished sniffing, we've work to do.'

Fanny realised that her tears had completely dried up, and she hadn't used her handkerchief in some minutes.

'What work?' she asked, confused.

'Well, I have no intention of handing over my two hundred pounds to the blackmailer tonight,' Aunt Jane said crisply. 'So we're going to trap her, you and I, and catch her in the act of trying to extort the money from you. And now we need to work out our plan.'

Fanny's jaw dropped. How in Heaven were they going to do that?

Chapter 29

The temple, Godmersham Park

The long grass was wet and cold and slippery from the rain. It slithered round Fanny's ankles like the tongues of eels. She stood close to the pillar of the temple and shrugged her cloak up around her neck. She prayed that the drizzle would let up.

This must be the miserable part of being a thief-taker, she thought.

It was very lonely, out here in the darkness. Fanny was trying not to lean against the comforting stone of the pillar because she knew it was covered in grimy lichen that would stain her rose-coloured cloak.

Even her beautiful cloak made her feel sad, for she knew Anna had a passion for it, and was jealous of it.

Anna had disappeared somewhere for the whole day. Fanny didn't know where she'd gone, and hadn't liked to ask.

Fanny had been playing billiards with George and Henry after dinner when Aunt Jane had come in and given her a significant look.

'No, no,' Henry had screamed. 'It's not bedtime yet!' He'd been winning the game, against his older brother too.

'All right, all right,' Aunt Jane had said vaguely. 'Not quite bedtime yet. I must steal Fanny away, though. She and I have business.'

Then they'd been passing through the door in the garden wall, and out into the dark of the park where the clouds were heavy with rain.

Fanny had made a slow circuit of the temple, wading through the grasses, to make sure that no one else was there yet, while Aunt Jane had melted away into the darkness of the bushes at the little building's rear, just as planned. Fanny would wait at the front so if the blackmailer did take the bait, she'd be clearly visible in the moonlight standing there all alone. Except there was no moon. The rain clouds had foiled that part of the plan.

Fanny's knees began to feel a bit shaky. She longed to

call out for Aunt Jane, and say that she could not go through with it. But the thought that her aunt would be disappointed braced her, and … so too did the thought of poor Mr Drummer, in prison, perhaps feeling cold and lonely himself.

Maybe fifteen minutes passed, agonisingly slowly, slower even than the deep tick of the clock in the marble hall of the house. Fanny started to daydream, just for a second, and then – inevitably – she was caught off guard when she heard what she'd been waiting for. It was the stealthy rustle of a person approaching through the grass. Oh! And that was the pinprick light of a lantern, wasn't it?

The beam of light illuminated strands of grass, then the leather of a pair of stout boots, and then breeches … this wasn't the shop woman from the draper's at all! It was a man!

Fanny took a great gulp of air into her lungs, ready to scream. This was someone who definitely shouldn't be here, in her father's park.

But she'd invited this stranger to come – hadn't she?

Her scream was stillborn in her throat. Was *this* in fact the blackmailer? What had she done?

Fanny froze, unsure whether to scream, or run, or keep her cool and challenge the intruder.

Think! she commanded herself. *What would a real thief-taker do?*

But the mysterious man decided for her.

He lifted his lantern, and now the pool of light travelled upward. A blue coat was revealed, and a long double row of buttons done up snugly round a swollen stomach. Then a necktie, and rather a florid face and … oh.

It was Mr Fortescue. Her father's fellow magistrate. He peered out at her from under the curls of his old-fashioned wig.

He snorted.

'So it's true!' he said. 'I would never have thought it of a Miss Austen. The gossip in the bar at the Star has revealed your plan, my dear. To buy the freedom of Dominic Drummer for two hundred pounds. This can't be done, you silly young pup. Not even ladies in love are above the law. And more to the point, and this is what I must have a word with your father about, where did you get that two hundred pounds? That's too much money for a young person to have got hold of honestly.'

Fanny's mouth opened and shut for a while, but no words came out. She was calculating what had happened. The draper's shop woman must have smelt a rat. She must have decided *not* to trust Fanny to bring the money to the temple as agreed. And she must have decided to turn Fanny in! She'd told Mr Fortescue the magistrate that Fanny would pay a bribe to get Dominic Drummer off!

Fanny's face felt hot. Would people think that she was so desperate for a husband that she'd try to buy one? With money that perhaps had been stolen?

She tried to speak, but her lips wouldn't move.

Oh, come on, she said to herself. Anna *wouldn't just stand about saying nothing.*

'Sir,' she pronounced at last, and she was pleased to hear that her voice was clear and steady. A gust of wind forced her to speak even louder, and that gave her more confidence.

'Sir, you are mistaken in your facts,' she said. 'I am not the wrongdoer here. I am trying to *catch* the blackmailer.'

Mr Fortescue gave a bark of laughter.

'Look here, Miss Fanny,' he said confidentially, stepping unpleasantly close to her. 'You're in trouble. Young misses in trouble are much better off telling the truth, rather than making up more crazy lies.'

Suddenly he swung his lantern away wildly, its beam dancing off across broken stems.

'Is that someone else?' he said urgently. 'Who's there?

Step forward! I am Mr Fortescue the magistrate. If you harm me, you will be pursued by officers of the law to the border of this county and beyond.'

Aunt Jane! It must be Aunt Jane. Fanny's heart rose. Her aunt would explain, get her out of this mess.

But that wasn't Aunt Jane coming out from behind the columns. It was – yes – it was her brother Edward, almost a grown man in the dim light, and rather ridiculously holding a sword. And then following him was her father, with Aunt Jane in the rear.

'Fortescue,' said Fanny's father. 'Unorthodox to meet like this.'

'Your daughter, the hussy,' said Mr Fortescue, taken aback, 'has been leading us a merry dance.'

Aunt Jane walked up close to him.

'You know, Mr Fortescue, there's a quick way to decide this,' she said.

Mr Fortescue was clearly not used to being forcefully advised by a lady in spectacles. He took a step back, unfortunately taking the lantern with him, so now Fanny and her family could not see each other. A shiver of wind lifted the hair on Fanny's neck.

Aunt Jane simply went on talking, raising her voice against the dark and windy night.

'Mr Fortescue!' she said. 'If Miss Fanny Austen has

come here to give a bribe, she will have two hundred pounds in her pocket. If, alternatively, she has come to catch a blackmailer in the act of extorting two hundred pounds – with myself, my brother and my nephew as her witnesses to her actions – then she will *not* have two hundred pounds in her pocket. Why don't you just look in her pocket?'

There was silence.

'Mr Austen?' Mr Fortescue asked.

'As my sister says, Fortescue,' Fanny's father responded.

Fanny stepped forward.

'If you would just hold the lantern still, sir,' she said crisply, 'I shall empty my pockets for you.' First, the pouch in the side of her cloak. Nothing but a handkerchief. Then the pocket she had tied on under her dress. Two shillings, the end of a pencil, and a small wooden horse.

'That belongs to my brother,' Fanny felt compelled to explain.

'Come on, Fortescue,' said Fanny's father, slapping him on the back. 'We'll go back to the house and explain. I think there's a nasty trick going on here, involving that draper's shop on the high street, and I believe that my parson, unfortunate fellow, is in the House of Correction on false evidence. My sister has taken me through it all this evening. And Fanny is a good-hearted girl.'

The two magistrates moved off down the hill, Fanny's father still talking and explaining. And in their wake, almost dizzy with relief, came Fanny. She occasionally stumbled in the grass, but Aunt Jane on one side, and Edward on the other, held on to her elbows.

'Good God,' said Edward, and neither Fanny nor Aunt Jane had the heart to reprove him for his blasphemy. 'You ladies have saved Mr Drummer. I didn't know you had it in you, Fan. You're fine fellows. Fine fellows!'

'If you're right, Austen,' Mr Fortescue was saying, 'it sounds like he's been hard done by. You'll have the young man back in the parish as soon as I can spring him from the gaol.'

A big foolish grin spread itself across Fanny's face as she saw the windows of the house come into view, and the glow of warmth and comfort from within.

There was only one thing missing to make her evening perfect. To be friends with Anna again.

Chapter 30

The glasshouse, Godmersham Park

But Fanny never really got the chance to speak to Anna before she left Godmersham.

Fanny's mother said that she and Anna still had to share a room, even after Mr Terry's departure, to save work for the maids. On each of the remaining nights of her stay, though, Anna refused to speak. She just crept into the bed and turned her face towards the wall, and lay there till morning. If Fanny woke in the night, she'd listen carefully for Anna's breathing.

Usually, she couldn't hear it, and she knew that Anna must be awake too, staring at nothing throughout the long hours of darkness.

So they never spoke of the horrible words Anna had

227

hurled, nor of Mr Terry. And Mr Drummer's name was certainly never mentioned between then, even though he had come back to the park, and been welcomed home with a party at which all of Fanny's brothers and sisters were present.

Anna stayed upstairs during the party, almost as if she couldn't bear to see other people having a good time.

When it was time to leave the mansion to go back to his parsonage, Mr Drummer took Fanny's hand in both of his, and held it for a long time without saying anything. He'd thanked her earlier, over and over again, but now he just stood there, looking into her eyes. He looked, and looked, until Fanny felt dizzy. She scarcely even heard the noise of the children all around them. Then he turned and went. And a few days later, Anna had gone too, wrapped in a big old black cloak and never once looking back as the carriage pulled away.

It was properly winter now, and the first frost had come to Godmersham. Fanny's mother had grown bigger in the belly, and ever slower at waddling round the house. She was scarcely to be seen outside her room, where it was unpleasantly hot. Fanny noticed that the goblets on the dinner table were growing smeary from being washed in cold water, and that the housemaids were leaving the grates dirty in the fireplaces.

Fanny decided that she ought to do something about the decay in the workings of the house, maybe at the very least to bring in some flowers. She thought she might use autumn leaves. It was the kind of fey touch her mother would never have allowed had she been feeling like herself.

But a cold morning out in the park picking up twigs of bronze and yellow foliage made Fanny feel alive and tingling round the ears. In the chilly greenhouse, unheated since the coal bill hadn't been paid, she tried to jam her pickings artistically into the vases. The dry dead leaves kept falling off their stems. *I must get Papa to give me a cheque for the coal merchant*, Fanny said to herself. *I know I can run the house perfectly well, I just need to be allowed to do it.*

'Lizzie!' she called, seeing her sister creeping past the glasshouse. 'Come in and help me! Where are you sneaking off to?'

Fanny could not help but think Lizzie had a guilty look about her. She wasn't dressed for outdoors, and came into the conservatory tugging her thin shawl round her thin shoulders. But her cheeks were ruddy, and she looked happy, not cold.

'Where *were* you off to?' Fanny asked again a few minutes later, having shoved a knife into Lizzie's hands, and having herself attacked the stems of some half-dead roses.

'Well, I was going to see Mr Drummer,' Lizzie conceded. That explained her lack of a jacket. His neat little parsonage was only a quarter of a mile down the drive, near the church, and it was hardly worth putting on a coat to get there on such a sunny day, even if it was raw and sharp.

Fanny pricked up her ears. She had such a possessive feeling about Mr Drummer, now merrily reinstalled as their neighbour, and preaching each Sunday to the assembled congregation from the estate. The forgiveness of sins was his favourite topic.

A pleasurable shiver ran down Fanny's spine at the memory of a secret smile he had given her from the pulpit, just two days ago.

Now that he was back, everything in the world seemed to be settling down the right way up again.

Everything, that is, except for Anna and her silence.

'And what did you want to talk to Mr Drummer about?' Fanny asked lightly. 'Have you sins to confess? You should tell your big sister if you have.'

To her surprise, Lizzie threw down the knife, and marched away to the other end of the conservatory. She stood there, hunched, looking out of a broken pane for several minutes, as if thinking something over.

Then, all of a sudden, she was back.

'I think I *will* tell you, Fan,' Lizzie said. 'I know you *can* keep a secret. Like when you caught the blackmailer with Aunt Jane. It was mean of you not to tell me about that.'

Fanny turned and leaned her back on the slate-topped counter. Lizzie had piqued her interest. What secrets could her little sister possibly have? Fanny was so used to telling Lizzie that no, she couldn't join her and Anna on a picnic, or no, she was too young to go out to a ball with them.

Soon she'll be out dancing too, Fanny thought. *People will expect me to try to find her partners.*

She'd been to hardly any balls since Anna's departure, making the excuse that her mother needed her at home. An excuse which wasn't quite true, Fanny realised, when she examined it more closely. Elizabeth didn't mind which of her daughters stayed with her. The truth was, as Lord Smedley had said, that Fanny only really wanted to dance with Mr Drummer.

But Lizzie was speaking now, and Fanny, unforgivably, hadn't been listening.

'What's that, Lizzie?' she was forced to ask. It was true that her sister was mumbling, addressing the knobbly cobbles of the glasshouse floor, which made her words hard to hear.

'Yes, I'm engaged,' she said, hanging her head.

Surely Fanny had misheard.

'I thought you said "engaged"!' she laughed. 'What did you really say?'

There was silence, just the nodding of Lizzie's head.

Now Fanny could see that there was a huge beaming smile trying to peep out from behind her sister's bashful expression.

Fanny's hand flew to her chest, and she tried to find something to say. But her lips were too cold to move.

She reached backwards, her hands catching on the edge of the slate top, which was unpleasantly wet.

Lizzie engaged before her! Fanny began to glimpse the humiliation that was in store for her as the older sister of a girl who wasn't even out in society, yet who'd stolen the prize of the first engagement.

At long last, after a pause that felt like an hour, Fanny realised what she ought to do. She stepped forward, opened her arms, and saw Lizzie's happy face for just a second before she disappeared into her sister's hug.

'Congratulations, Lizzie!' Fanny whispered into her

sister's hair. 'Oh, congratulations! But who are you engaged to?'

Lizzie pulled away, incredulous.

'Oh, Fanny,' she said. 'Who did you think? To Christopher, of course.'

Fanny smiled again, with a bit more warmth. Of course! Lizzie was engaged to Christopher Hurst, whom the whole family had known forever.

Christopher, from Hurstbourne House in the next village, whose father had land just like Mr Austen did, and with whom Edward went hunting and with whom Lizzie rode to hounds too whenever she could get her father to let her take out a horse.

But once again, Fanny had the sensation of being left sitting on the shelf. Were all the girls in the family going to find a husband before she did? Mr Drummer had been back at Godmersham for some weeks now. There'd be no need to worry about what her parents might say if the question of marriage never came up at all.

That was two engagements achieved within the family, and neither of them for Fanny.

Chapter 31

The parsonage, Godmersham Park

Lizzie's engagement did not receive quite such a warm welcome at Godmersham Park as Anna's had done a couple of months earlier.

'Oh Lord, Lizzie, are you sure?' were their mother Elizabeth's words.

This was after Fanny had persuaded Lizzie to go back into the house with her and spill her secret to their parents. But it turned out that Christopher had done things exactly by the book, consulting Edward in private, receiving his paternal encouragement to ask Lizzie herself, and taking every step strictly in order.

Yet that evening, Fanny overheard her mother and

Aunt Jane quietly discussing the engagement on the sofa in the library.

'She's so very young,' Aunt Jane was saying. 'It will have to be a long engagement. And do you think she truly knows her own mind?'

They'd broken off when they saw that Fanny was near, and once again she felt excluded. Lizzie, just like Anna, would now be drawn into the confidential conversation of the adult ladies, while Fanny was left to play nursemaid to the younger children.

By the afternoon of the next day, Fanny found herself trotting down the drive to the parsonage. She really wanted to talk about Lizzie's engagement with a friend. *And Mr Drummer is a* family *friend*, Fanny told herself, severely.

Yet she'd neglected to tell anyone where she was going.

But Fanny now realised, as she jogged along, that she couldn't really talk about Lizzie, as the engagement was not yet generally known. Perhaps she could ask whether Mr Drummer's housekeeper could oblige with some sausages for the Godmersham dinner, which would otherwise be just potatoes. The butcher had refused to send any more meat until his account had been settled.

Mr Drummer's housekeeper welcomed Fanny on the doorstep of the parsonage. She was a regular visitor, and she and her sisters often drank tea in the little house's little parlour. Its fire was kept burning day-long while Mr Drummer composed his sermons at the gate-leg table by the window. He seemed to spend an awfully long time doing it, and Fanny's sisters laughed at him for his slowness.

On her previous visit, though, Fanny had learned that he was doing something more significant than just writing the next week's address to his parishioners.

'I'm trying to polish up the poems I wrote when I was – ahem – in the House of Correction,' he'd explained when she'd glanced at the table and asked why his sermon had such short lines of text.

Of course, she'd known he liked books. That had been one of the first conversations they'd had. But Fanny hadn't realised just how seriously he took them.

'And are you talented in the literary department yourself, Miss Austen?' he'd asked, seeing her look of pleasure. 'Perhaps … like some other members of your family?'

All at once, Fanny had realised that he knew the secret of how her aunt Jane spent her time.

'No, no,' she'd said, quickly, 'I'd like to try, but I haven't the courage. But I admire those who do. Especially those who earn a living from their pens. Why do you smile?'

'Because, Miss Austen,' he'd said, 'if I may be so bold, a young lady who is known in these parts as a thief-taker can hardly lack the courage to pick up a pen and put it to paper.'

Fanny could all too well imagine her mother's dismayed reaction to any suggestion that she might try her hand at writing anything.

Mr Drummer seemed to think it was easy, but he couldn't possibly know what it was like to be a Miss Austen of Godmersham, with all its odd restrictions on what you could and couldn't do. Unless perhaps she could explain it to him one day?

But now, in the parlour, he was heaving a histrionic sigh as he put away the pages of his work into a folder.

'I would so like to supplement my income by my pen,' he admitted after greeting Fanny.

'And ... may I say this?' he added, pushing his folder away and turning toward the teapot. 'I hope it does not offend if I say that your aunt has been a great inspiration for me in that regard.'

Fanny had been sitting down on the hearthrug since Mrs Heathcote left the room after bringing in the tea. Of course, the housekeeper had carefully left the door open to preserve propriety. Fanny nevertheless turned her head sharply towards it.

What if Mrs Heathcote were still in the hall? This was the darkest of secrets, her aunt had made her promise never to tell. But Mr Drummer seemed to be in her aunt's confidence already!

'Tell me,' she asked in a rush, drawing up her knees to her chin and wrapping her arms around them. 'There's one thing I've never understood. How it is that you know Aunt Jane?'

'Well,' he said, smiling at her solemnly, 'I read a marvellous book. *Pride and Prejudice*. We spoke about it before. So, I wrote to the author, at the address of the publisher, a long letter saying what I liked about it and how clever I thought it, and saying a few words about my own position as a young curate with good intentions but no situation. And to my surprise, I got a letter back. It was not only from the author herself, whose … sex … was quite other than I had imagined, but it also contained a most kind, most generous, offer of a post. She said she thought she might enjoy – as she put it – having a literary parson.'

He looked intently at Fanny, and must have seen that he was saying nothing that she hadn't begun to deduce for herself.

'And was it …' she began.

'Yes, it was,' he said simultaneously.

'… Aunt Jane!'

Fanny leaped to her feet, and almost clapped her hands.

'Oh, that's why it all happened,' she said. 'Aunt Jane is so mysterious. She never explains anything. I'm sure you know that my family don't know that she writes books. They just think she's a bit clever and odd.'

'Quite right of her not to tell them,' he said seriously. 'A lady who writes may draw the wrong sort of attention to herself. As may a clergyman who dabbles in inky pleasures. Perhaps I should desist since I'm safely back on solid ground.'

He looked down so sadly at his unfinished poem that Fanny longed to squeeze his shoulders to cheer him up, as she might have done if it were one of her brothers who couldn't finish his school lesson.

'Oh, but you have talent,' she said. 'I'm sure of it. You must follow my aunt's example, and work away!'

He didn't look up, but Fanny could tell that a blush was mounting up his throat.

At that moment, she wished with her whole heart that he could become a published author. Nothing seemed more desirable.

'Your encouragement means a great deal, Miss Austen,' he softly said.

Chapter 32

The town hall, Canterbury

The roar from within the courtroom was audible
even on the street. The sound seemed to come out
through the gloomy doorway to fight with the
other noises of the Canterbury marketplace, where sheep
were bleating, servants who wanted masters were calling out their skills, and the women selling loaves and
apples were almost screaming out their bargain prices.

James handed Fanny out of the coach and paused,
standing before her, blocking her way. She realised, to
her surprise, that for once he was looking her in the eye.

'Good luck, miss,' he said.

The unexpected kindness made Fanny gulp. It also
reminded her of the ordeal that lay ahead, and she

straightened her shoulders. She tried to look as tall as Aunt Jane.

'Thank you!'

But of course, she wasn't going to be alone. Mr Drummer would be right there behind her.

'Miss Austen, if you require them, I have smelling salts in my pocket,' Mr Drummer announced. 'Just say the word.'

She smiled. It was a bit nanny-ish of him, but it was awfully sweet. Emboldened, she stepped towards the town hall's great door as if she were the finest lady in London town. Only on the inside was she still quaking.

The letter from Mr Sprack had arrived the week after Lizzie's engagement. Aunt Jane had called Fanny into her room to read it to her privately.

'No need to tell your parents,' she'd said, peering at Fanny over her reading glasses. 'I'm sure they wouldn't want you to give evidence in the public court. But Mr Sprack writes that a prestidigitarian, a woman, has been captured. He thinks that she might be the one employed in the draper's shop in Canterbury, the one who planted the lace on Mr Drummer. The problem is that she will need to be identified in court.'

'You mean,' Fanny had asked, 'that *I* might have to identify her? As the woman who showed me the lace?

The one who said that if I gave her the money Mr Drummer could walk free?'

'And your Mr Drummer, too, ideally,' Aunt Jane had said.

To Fanny's surprise, she wasn't at first daunted by the prospect. Her mind had somehow jumped immediately to the thought of travelling to Canterbury in the carriage with Mr Drummer. A courtroom, a judge, bearing witness: all had the power to make her feel sick. But surely she and Mr Drummer would have to travel together to get there. Everyone knew that it was improper for a young lady to ride with a young man, unless of course the circumstances made it unavoidable. It was an exciting thought.

And the day had come. The carriage ride had been blissful, even if the conversation had been utterly proper for parson and parishioner. But now the treat was over and the awful part had arrived. Fanny had to force her feet to carry her over the town hall's threshold.

Inside, the officers were calling for order. It was with extreme reluctance that the crowd packing out the spectators' benches began to quieten down.

As she made her way forward, Fanny could feel that the eyes of the pack, every one of them, were on her bonnet, her gown, her figure.

She folded her gloved hands before her, and inched her way towards the front.

This is no good! said a little voice inside her head. Anna, for instance, would never mince into a court-room in such a half-ashamed manner. And she wanted Mr Drummer, walking behind her, to think her brave and bold.

So instead she put up her head, and stepped up smartly to the table before the judge.

To her left, she recognised the warder from the House of Correction.

And next to him stood a woman, in the grubby-looking grey gown of that place, with her hair ragged and her face dirty.

'Miss Austen of Godmersham Park!'

She heard the intake of breath in the crowded court, and once again felt wobbly as jelly. Yes, she had the protection of her father's name and the name of her home. But if he actually knew that she was here, doing this, he would be furious.

And her mother, well, she couldn't even begin to think of what her mother would say.

A black-suited gentleman was showing her where to stand, how to raise her hand for the oath.

Who in Kent would marry a girl who had made such

a public performance of herself? The treacherous voice in her head took on her mother's tones.

Then the answer came. Well, a man like Dominic Drummer might, and there he was standing right behind her. Anna came into Fanny's mind as well. Yes, Anna, even though she was no longer Fanny's cousin, would be proud to stand up and see justice done. And so, of course, would Aunt Jane and Mr Sprack. That was why they did their mysterious work.

And justice *would* be done.

Fanny knew it at once, even if the knowledge made her take a deep and desperate breath. For she'd caught the eye of the woman in grey. She knew at once, immediately, and without doubt, that it was the same person from the shop.

But now, and to her horror, a flicker of something else, something unidentifiable, ran through Fanny's body. Pity? Yes, it was pity. Fanny felt sorry for the woman, who looked defiant and miserable at the same time.

Fanny knew all too well what it was like in that terrible House of Correction. She could only imagine how much worse it would be on the ship to Australia.

'Do you see here present in the court the person who offered to pervert the course of justice for money?'

Fanny looked at the lawyer who was asking her, then

again at the woman, who was now staring straight ahead of her.

Oh, but this was even harder than Fanny had expected. Why had the woman needed the money? Did she perhaps have hungry children to feed? How much Fanny herself had in the world, and this grubby woman, how little. She had not considered this aspect of being a thief-taker. She had not considered this *at all*.

Fanny opened her mouth, but no words came out.

Eventually, she remembered how the woman had been quite happy for Mr Drummer to go to Australia. It did the trick.

From the soles of her feet, Fanny summoned up a little voice.

'Yes, it is,' she said. 'I can confirm that this was the woman. And if you look closely at her left thumb, you will see she has a wart there.'

The courtroom throbbed with a thunderous murmuring, and the lawyer smacked his hands on the table with satisfaction. The nasty warder from the House of Correction jerked the woman's arm behind her back. And the woman herself turned straight towards Fanny, aiming a shiny great gob of her spit to go flying through the air.

It fell short, but even so Fanny turned away in

disgust, almost falling over a chair. It was so noisy. The faces of the crowd were almost spinning about her.

Now it was Mr Drummer who gently shoved her downwards towards the chair, and whispered in her ear, putting his lips so near that Fanny could hear him despite the hubbub.

'It's over,' he said. 'Well done.'

For the first time in her life, perhaps, Fanny felt she'd done something that could almost be described as heroic.

Chapter 33

The parsonage, Godmersham Park

After the unsettling business of being a witness in court, and what was almost worse, the fury of her parents when they heard about it afterwards, Fanny found herself strolling towards the parsonage even more frequently than before.

Just, of course, to consult her spiritual adviser. Mr Drummer scrupulously kept the door open, and never again talked of Aunt Jane or other secrets. But there was plenty else to discuss. Fanny needed to talk, quite often it seemed, about whether it was right or wrong to send women as well as men to Australia, and whether the present system of unpaid magistrates was satisfactory for administering the law of the land. She also still longed to talk about whether her sister Lizzie might not be too young to be engaged.

Fanny had more than once overheard her parents arguing about the engagement. Why had her father not consulted her? her mother had yelled. Because she was so busy, too busy, her father stormed in reply, never able to listen to a single word he had to say because she was busy with all the blasted children. And now she could scarcely get out of bed because of the new baby expected at any moment.

'And whose fault is that, Mr Austen?' Fanny's mother had yelled back.

Fanny also feared that once again, just as with Anna, her father had perhaps said yes to Lizzie's engagement partly because he was simply too genial, too lazy, and too eager to please other people to have given the decision the thought it deserved. He'd just assumed that his wife – as she'd so often said – would be only too glad to see a daughter married.

What would Mr Drummer say? Would he agree that Lizzie was just a little too young to know her own mind? Fanny quickened her step. It would be so pleasurable, one day, to use words like 'engagement' and 'marriage' in his company.

In the neat little garden at the side of his house,

Mr Drummer was working away in his shirtsleeves with a shovel, rootling about for potatoes.

'Ah,' he said. 'I'm not ashamed for you to see me doing this, Miss Austen. Of course you know I have no gardener. Not the same with Mrs Hurst, who just came to call. She managed to suggest without quite saying it that it's undignified for me to look after my own vegetables.'

'How ridiculous!' Fanny said. 'I knew those Hursts had delusions of grandeur.'

She wanted to ask Mr Drummer if she thought that Lizzie would be happy as part of a family that took itself as seriously as her own Austen family did, with all the trials that brought her. But perhaps that was a bit too … much.

He'd wonder what she'd come for, Fanny fretted, shifting her weight from foot to foot, if she didn't have anything to say now she was here.

Yet he seemed perfectly satisfied with her presence.

'Come inside,' he said. 'It's time for tea.'

In the drawing room, he ceremoniously took her cashmere shawl from her, and kept it on his knee, stroking and admiring it. Fanny occupied herself with stirring up the coals a little.

It occurred to her that she had perhaps taken rather

too much upon herself, to treat his poker like this as if it were her own.

She quickly sat down on the hearthrug.

To her surprise, Mr Drummer began to open up the main matter of the moment.

'And now, Miss Austen,' he said, 'after Mrs Hurst's call, I believe that the happy news in the Godmersham family is public knowledge.'

Of course. Of course, Mrs Hurst had paid the call to gossip and show off about an engagement. Fanny's stomach tensed up.

Mrs Hurst must be visiting all her neighbours, and saying, 'Of course, it's not right that the younger Miss Austen should be married before the elder. But Miss Fanny has been out in society for nearly a whole year, you know. Let me see, do we know any suitable young men for her? The family at Godmersham are really quite genteel ...'

Fanny grew so lost in imagining the scene that she hardly listened to what Mr Drummer was saying.

To her surprise, he was down at her level, on his hands and knees on the hearthrug too, tilting his head to see into her face.

His eyes held a tender, quizzical expression of concern.

All at once she had a premonition of what was about to happen.

Was this delightful, or horrible, or both? Shivery feelings began to run up and down Fanny's wrists. Even her spine began to tingle.

He coughed gently, and hung his head, so that he addressed her slippers.

Fanny noticed, at this important moment, the very stupid fact that the rug had a worn patch where the old parson's tea table had stood.

'Miss Austen,' he was saying urgently. 'It could be a ... double wedding, you know. I would be only too honoured to speak to your father if, I mean, if I could believe that your feelings would allow you to welcome such a move.'

She saw then that he was kneeling shakily on the rug before her, while the tufts of his hair on the crown of his head quivered.

He's as nervous as I am! she thought.

But his nervousness also created a warm, protective glow inside her. He *always* seemed to give her such a feeling, at the ball, in the prison, now in his own drawing room.

As soon as he'd spoken, Fanny glanced involuntarily at the door. Here she was being proposed to! Surely this was a proposal? It wasn't what she'd expected. She'd never pictured it like this. She'd imagined moonlight, or a garden, not just sitting on a rug.

What would her parents say?

Fanny simply didn't know what to think. Sweet, charming, docile Mr Drummer. Why wasn't she happy? Wouldn't she be happy with him? Why was it not … sweeter?

But surely, surely, this was exactly what she'd been waiting for. Yes, this is what she'd wanted. She'd dreamed of this moment!

'Thank you,' she panted. 'But I must just speak to my father first, before I reply, reply formally I mean.' Unceremoniously, she bolted out of the room. A concoction of pride and shame gave wings to her feet.

'Sorry!' she called back through the door. 'I must just fix something first, before you do, speak to Papa, I mean.'

He was on his feet too, and bowing, and saying of course, she should think things over, take some time, but what about her …

She did not stay to listen. She was flying, flying up the drive. She knew exactly what she had to do: find her father. She needed to confront him, like she had that time before in the library, and to tell him that she'd made her choice, and that she demanded his approval.

She was back in the house before she realised that in her haste and confusion and tumult she must have failed to hear Dominic warning her that she'd left her best shawl behind.

Chapter 34

Upstairs

Why was it so quiet within the house?

That was Fanny's first thought after she'd hurled herself through the door in the garden wall and in through the side door and on into the marble hall, where her slippers were leaving little bits of wet grass on the floor.

Despite having just received a proposal, she bent to pick up the mess. She couldn't *not* do something like that.

All the time she did so, Mr Drummer's unexpected words were ringing in her ears. 'Honoured,' he'd said. 'Your feelings,' he'd said.

She hadn't thought it would be like this. She'd thought

that her feelings would be bigger, more unmanageable. But she was determined to find her father at once and get on with it. Where was he? Where was Aunt Jane?

Oh, but this was silly, Fanny thought, having looked into the quiet drawing room and then the empty library. Long oblongs of light from the late-afternoon sun were fading on the carpets. Everyone had disappeared, and Fanny noticed that both fires had died down. Clearly, no one had been attending to them. The house was going to pieces.

She sighed, and set to work poking the drawing-room fire back into life. Soon it would be time for her to pour out the tea, as she'd done since their mother retreated upstairs. But making a fire! Pouring the tea! It wasn't exactly an ordeal. Fanny had felt a lot luckier in her life since she had been to the House of Correction. She knew she had so much more than many other people; she had sent a woman to Australia. Compared to that, her life was easy.

Holding the poker reminded her of the much smaller fireplace at the parsonage. And there again in her head was Mr Drummer, Mr Dominic Drummer. She finally had a proper suitor of her own ... But was he *extraordinary*? Or was he only just *good enough*? Would he win

256

the support of Aunt Jane, whose approval would be necessary if her father made a fuss? And Aunt Jane had always been so impenetrable!

Fanny's impatience to get on with the task of speaking to her father made her almost whimper out loud. She decided to venture upstairs. The stairs were strewn with the children's toys, a discarded hobbyhorse; a spinning top. And a whip! Fanny picked it up, tutting with annoyance. It was dangerous, people might fall over it.

Now she could hear voices, and Louie's thin high wail.

At last. So, everyone was up here.

Fanny was sighing loudly as she set off along the wide corridor towards her mother's room. But she was only halfway there when its door burst open. And there stood Aunt Jane, wiping her hands on a napkin. She wiped and wiped, as if her hands were very dirty.

Fanny could not look away. It seemed, no, it couldn't be … but it did seem as if her aunt's hands were coated in something red. Something like blood.

'Fanny,' Aunt Jane said, 'thank goodness you're here. Lord knows where my brother Edward has gone out to, and Mrs Sackree most unfortunately is in Canterbury this afternoon.'

Fanny snapped shut the lips she had opened to tell

Aunt Jane that something had happened. Something important, for once in her life.

Aunt Jane noticed.

'Later, Fanny,' she said. 'Later. It's important that you must be brave now. You must be a heroine. You must take your brothers and sisters downstairs, and keep them busy. They shouldn't be in here. They mustn't be in here.'

At her words, Louie came out of their mother's bedroom, bawling, her face just a great wet mess of tears. In her wake came Henry, carrying baby Cassie, and looking very pale and serious.

'Children!' called Aunt Jane furiously. 'Go downstairs at once with Fanny, now. At once.' She plunged back inside, and Fanny could hear a strange, frightening sound from within, not a child's wail, but a horrible panting, breathy, continuous scream.

The little ones came spilling out of the room, and last of all came Lizzie.

'Our new baby brother is coming out too soon,' she said to Fanny. She was breathing far too fast, and had to gasp out the words. 'There's no one here to help. No one! Take them down at once, find the grooms, find somebody. And get the blood off them. And get the doctor!'

Fanny's slow brain realised that the awful sound was being made by their mother.

Lizzie and Aunt Jane stared at her fiercely. The children cried.

'Go, Fanny, go,' said Aunt Jane. 'Think of your brothers and sisters now. It's important.'

Fanny took a deep breath. It was all so … unexpected. She felt dizzy at the completely horrifying and unbelievable sight of a speck of red on Cassie's bib.

'Oh, Cassie,' she said, sadly. 'Let me take that off you. And we'll go downstairs. Everything will be all right downstairs. Come on Henry,' she said, 'there's a fire in the drawing room.'

What a ridiculous, nonsensical thing to say, she told herself, when their mother was ill and needed a doctor. As if anyone cared if there was a fire!

But she could see that the little children weren't taking in her words, just the normal sound of her voice.

'Mama!' cried Louie again. 'Her stomach is sick!'

'Shut up, Louie,' said George fiercely. 'Shut up! Shut up!'

'Come on, everyone,' said Fanny. 'Let's just go down, shall we? And Henry? Can you run, as fast as you can, to the stable, and find James, and tell him to go to town to fetch the doctor? At once, Henry, at once! And Henry, if

James isn't there, run down the road to Mr Drummer. Yes, you can. Stop crying, look at me, I'm not crying, am I? Yes, off you go.'

Fanny herded the smaller children into the drawing room, and fetched the hobbyhorse, and the top and whip, a game that wasn't normally allowed in that particular room, and soon they were all playing, in an echo of their normal life. Fanny kept asking them questions, and telling them that their mother would be well just as soon as the doctor came, and that he was coming very soon.

In her heart, though, a black feeling was gathering.

The sound of a vehicle on the gravel drew them all to the window. But it wasn't Doctor Jackson's high gig with its enormous wheels. It was just the farm wagon, bringing back the servants who'd been into town for their holiday.

Even so, Fanny was consumed with a huge flooding feeling of relief.

'Just wait here,' she commanded her siblings. 'Mrs Sackree's coming. Look, there she is, getting out of the wagon!'

She darted out of the room and hared up the staircase. Now, at last, she could see her mother.

The corridor was growing dim as the afternoon was

nearly over, and at first Fanny didn't see the strange huddled shape against the wall.

She lurched forward, trying to make it out.

It was two people, sitting on the floor.

Aunt Jane had her arm round Lizzie's shoulders, and Lizzie's face was white and her eyes had an odd stare. She lifted her finger to her lips.

'Quiet, Fanny,' she hissed. 'Mama is sleeping at last. We were just about to creep downstairs to tell you. We didn't want to make a noise. Be very quiet, don't disturb her.'

Fanny moved towards the door.

'No!' said Lizzie, almost crossly. 'Don't go in. She's sleeping, I tell you!'

Something wasn't right.

Fanny looked at Aunt Jane, who was sadly shaking her head and hugging Lizzie. Aunt Jane's sleeves were still rolled up so that her long pale forearms glimmered in the half-light as she moved.

'Your mama will be sleeping, Fanny,' Aunt Jane said quietly, 'for a very long time indeed.'

Chapter 35

The library, Godmersham Park

Although they still lived in exactly the same house, everything was different. Godmersham Park had become a dark, sombre, quiet place. A place where, if the children made a noise, Fanny's father shouted so angrily they shrank into frightened silence.

Although he was present, he seemed to have travelled a long, long way away from them. It was weeks, it seemed, before Fanny even found herself in the same room as her father.

And the clockwork mechanism which had once seemed to run Godmersham Park had completely fallen apart. After her mother's death, Fanny simply had no time to feel sorrow. She and Aunt Jane were just too busy looking after her nine brothers and sisters, and the new one, the tiny baby John whose birth had hurt Fanny's mother so much.

Some of the maids had left, one of them saying that she didn't want the bad luck of living in a house where the mistress had died. The rest were demoralised. Fires went unlit, bathwater was cold, the meals were inedible.

Mrs Sackree and Aunt Jane and Fanny herself were in charge now.

So this *is why my mother never had any time*, Fanny thought, running from room to room. *And how much of it I used to have! How I used to waste it.*

Fanny had always wanted to be one of the grown-ups, she remembered, as she got up once more in the early hours to comfort little wailing John. And now, she told herself bitterly, she'd got her heart's desire.

The little children were sad and lost, the big children sullen and angry. Fanny tried to organise them into shuttle-cock, or bowls. They would play for a while, absorbed in their toys for a few minutes, then someone would fall over, someone would start crying, someone else would call for Mama, and it would all begin again.

The next day following the disaster, Mr Drummer of course came to the house. He was, after all, their parson, and couldn't stay away, Fanny told herself. But she didn't want to see him and stayed upstairs. It was all too much to have to think about what he'd asked her.

But after a while, Aunt Jane's head on its long neck poked itself round the door of Fanny's room.

'Mr Dominic Drummer,' she said, 'insisted on coming upstairs. He's right here in the passage. Fanny! Have you got anything to say to him?'

As the door was open, Fanny knew that he could hear. She spoke clearly and loudly.

'Aunt Jane,' she said, 'please tell Mr Drummer that I ... have to think of my brothers and sisters now. Much as I may want to, I can't ... I can't ...'

Fanny's voice petered out and she couldn't say anything more. A wave of pain seemed to break over her head.

Aunt Jane and Fanny looked at each other, silent, aghast. Then there was the sound of someone walking away from the door, and very quietly, very gently, going down the stairs.

'I think he understands,' said Aunt Jane, sadly. 'He was a nice young man.'

Fanny went into her mother's room, and smushed her face into the cold mattress that was the only thing left behind on Elizabeth's stripped bed, and cried.

All this time Fanny's father was horrifically busy,

dealing with the coffin maker, and going into town to report the death, and also trying to get together the cash to pay for the farm workers and the fees and the funeral.

But finally, one evening, Fanny was sitting stiff as a wooden doll on a chair in the library. She was too tired to go upstairs to bed, although she knew that she ought to. It was late when her father came in.

He was carrying a candle and looked like he was on his own way to bed.

'Fanny,' he said expressionlessly, going to his desk and starting to search for something there.

Fanny said nothing. She hadn't the heart.

Perhaps if she'd said 'Good evening, Papa' in her normal polite manner, he would have just gone on his way. But she didn't.

He stopped, and looked at her, and it was as if he was recognising an old friend he'd once known.

'Fanny!' he said, again, and put down his candle. Fanny came back to life, and stood up to give him the sort of hug she hadn't had since she'd been a tiny girl. Since the time when she'd been the only Austen in the nursery, not just the first of eleven.

'You must be their mother now, Fanny,' Edward said.

Fanny mutely nodded. She knew it. Yes, she had responsibilities now, and oh, how heavily they weighed.

265

There wasn't a single second now to think about balls, or beaux.

Perhaps this was what it was like for Anna's step-mother, Mary, trying to run a house on what seemed like not enough money.

'Jane says,' her father mumbled into Fanny's hair, 'that you are the best mother the children could have.'

'Really?'

Fanny's heart grew lighter, a little more luminous, at the thought Aunt Jane had said such a thing about her.

His big body gave a great heave, and Fanny could feel that he was letting out a sob. Of course, her father would go to pieces without his wife to nag him and console him, even though he'd complained about her – or so it had seemed – every single day of their life. Fanny real-ised that she could have predicted that he would.

After all, they had loved each other.

'My dearest Elizabeth and I were wrong,' her father said, 'to make it seem like we wanted to get rid of you, to get you married off. We must have been mad.'

Fanny nodded, feeling about a million years old.

The idea that she and Anna had been completely obsessed with themselves and their future lives during her mother's last few months pained Fanny almost more than anything else.

She remembered how desperate she had been to leave her mother behind. *When all the time*, Fanny thought, *I didn't know that she was going to be leaving me.*

A great gush of grief ran through her, then drained away.

'That's right,' she agreed out loud with her father. 'It wasn't so important after all.' She felt a tiny bit better.

Her brothers and sisters must never be allowed to feel, like Anna, that they didn't have a mother. And what might happen to her father as a widower? He needed so much, company, reassurance, bustle all around him.

But she would worry about that tomorrow. Tonight, at least, she knew what her future held. Tonight, at last, she'd be able to sleep peacefully.

Chapter 36

Return to Godmersham Park

It had not been possible for Anna to come to Kent in time for her aunt Elizabeth's funeral. But within the month, the entire Hampshire Austen family from Steventon were expected at Godmersham for a visit.

Fanny was feeling strange, oh, so strange, at the thought of seeing Anna.

Before her mother's death she would have sworn that she and Anna could never, ever have made it up. Not after what Anna had said.

But now everything was changed. Fanny was longing to see her cousin again more than almost anything in the world.

Fanny felt different, and she was aware that even

Godmersham itself was different. Shabbier, perhaps. Sadder, definitely.

She wiped her hands on the apron that she now wore practically all the time, scarcely ever taking it off. Her brothers and sisters were so messy. And she'd had to work out all the different charities her mother gave money to, all the workers the house employed, all the responsibilities.

And yet, as she lined her siblings up on the gravel to greet their uncle and aunt and cousin, Fanny felt a certain glow of pride. Their faces were clean, they were dressed mainly in clean clothes, and they were all present and correct – except for tiny baby John. She had done that.

She imagined their mama looking down on all the children from the window of her bedroom above, and saying, 'Well done, Fan. You've worked hard and organised everything. I knew you'd be good at this.'

But when she remembered once again who was about to arrive, the pinpricks of anxiety returned.

There wasn't time to get any more nervous, though, for here was the rumble of the carriage wheels. To Fanny's horror, Louie had started crying, spoiling the scrubbed-face, clean-clothed line-up. But then, after all, it didn't matter a jot because her uncle James, and Anna, and Aunt Mary were unpacking themselves from the carriage.

Within two seconds, Anna was giving Fanny a hug. Tears were spilling down her cheeks, almost like a river, almost as if Elizabeth had only just died.

Anna felt like the one person on earth who might truly understand Fanny's loss.

'I'm sorry, Fanny,' Anna was saying, holding Fanny in a strong grip, as strong as a lion of the desert. 'I'm sorry for everything.'

Fanny understood that Anna wasn't just talking about her aunt Elizabeth. She was also apologising for the quarrel.

Half an hour later, Anna, Fanny and Aunt Jane were having a quiet, grown-up tea party in Aunt Jane's room. Anna's stepmother had taken charge of the younger children so that Mrs Sackree could have a rest.

'So?' asked Aunt Jane, as the cups were filled for the second time. 'It's all right for us to talk about something else than Aunt Elizabeth, you know. We have talked about her for a long time. And I think that you, Anna, have something to tell us.'

Fanny looked at Anna.

Yes, it must be true. Anna's cheeks were smeary, as

they'd all been crying, but there was something a bit different about her. Her face seemed thinner and paler, but she was perhaps calmer, more sure of herself than before.

She's become a heroine, just like Aunt Jane said, Fanny thought.

It was so funny not to have seen Anna for such a long time that she'd physically changed. Perhaps Fanny should have noticed it sooner.

'You know, Anna,' she said in a rush, 'I never really thought before what it was like for you not having a mother of your own.'

Anna looked down at the floor.

She didn't smile, but she did look … content.

'Yes,' she said. 'It's difficult. But I've found a way. And my way is this. I want to tell you, Fanny, what Aunt Jane already knows.'

Fanny frowned. Had Anna written to Aunt Jane instead of herself with news, something from which Fanny had been excluded?

Fanny realised, suddenly, that her own stupid pride had prevented her from writing to Anna with the news of her mother's death. She'd left it to her father to inform Uncle James. She couldn't complain.

'Yes,' said Anna. 'I am engaged.'

Fanny's hands flew to her cheeks and her mouth formed an O of surprise.

'Good Lord, I hope not to Mr Terry!' she said at once, before clapping her hand over her open mouth.

What had she said? If Mr Terry was inexplicably back in favour – and Anna was capable of anything, really – then she'd made a terrible error in expressing her thoughts so clearly.

'No, no,' said Anna, half laughing, half crying, 'not Mr Terry. Good Lord! No, that was a very silly mistake. I'm to be the wife of another clergyman, though. Mr Lefroy.'

Fanny had heard the name before. Yes, there was a family of that name near Steventon. Anna had spoken of them previously. Fanny knew at once what her duty required.

'Anna,' she said at once, sternly, bracing herself to do it immediately, 'do you love him? Will you *die* if you *don't* marry him? Do you know what you are doing, this time?'

Anna smiled again, but sadly.

'I *do* love him,' she said quietly, but firmly. 'Perhaps not passionately, but I do. Also, Fanny, he will give me a future. I need to leave home,' she said. 'I can't bear it there any longer.'

The quiet desperation in her voice nearly broke Fanny's heart.

Fanny suddenly realised that Aunt Jane was standing with her hand on Anna's shoulder.

'Nobody is right and nobody is wrong,' Aunt Jane said authoritatively. 'For Anna, the best thing is to marry this man who seems honourable, and who can give her a better life. But Fanny will be like a mother to her brothers and sisters. I'm very proud of my nieces, who are both heroines.'

Fanny turned to Anna, and just like old times, gave her a shy little smile.

Chapter 37

The library, Godmersham Park

It had been an afternoon of snow, then the clouds had parted and the late low sun had come out and turned the park a pale pink. And now fat snowflakes were falling again, out of what looked like a clear sky.

All through tea, the great topic of conversation had been whether the snow would prevent the carriages from getting to tonight's ball at Hurstbourne House.

Anna and her parents had gone back to Steventon, and the evening had arrived when Lizzie was to be the belle of a ball her new family were holding to celebrate her engagement to their son.

Although Marianne had begged and begged to be allowed to go, Fanny had held firm.

'But it's nearly Christmas,' Marianne had wailed, dredging up yet one more excuse.

'It makes no difference, Marianne,' Fanny said. 'You haven't gained a year in age, have you, since we last discussed this ten minutes ago? The fact remains that you are too young. Too young to go out to balls!'

'Too young to go husband-hunting,' added Aunt Jane.

'Mother says it's *never* too young to begin planning if you want to make a good marriage,' Marianne replied, smartly.

Silence fell in the room. Marianne, aghast, clapped her hands over her mouth.

'Oh,' she wailed. 'For one minute I forgot.'

She stormed out of the room, tears flowing. Lizzie sighed, got to her feet, and followed.

'I need to go up and dress anyway,' she said. 'I'll get her to help me with my gown. She'll like that. Unless you'd rather, Fanny?'

Fanny did rather want the fun of dressing up Lizzie like a doll, but she realised that the little girls would enjoy it even more. She smiled and shook her head.

There was a noisy exodus from the library, all the children storming upstairs either to comfort Marianne or to 'help' Lizzie, or possibly just to get in the way.

After a short pause, the door opened once again, and Lizzie's face popped back into view.

'Fanny,' she said, 'it's not too late for you to decide that you do want to come after all. Change your mind?'

Fanny sighed, and smiled.

'No, thank you,' she said. 'You know that all your friends will be there. I think you'll have a fine time.'

'I know I will,' Lizzie declared, but she sounded doubtful. 'It's just that there's that first agonising bit of going into the ballroom and everyone looking at you, you know. Just that very first moment.'

'If he's worth anything at all, Christopher will look after you,' Fanny said. She remembered her own first ball at the Star Inn, and how it hadn't been that awful after all. And then Lizzie was grinning, and gone, flying off back upstairs.

Fanny and Aunt Jane were left in sudden silence, sitting either side of the fire, looking across it at each other and each holding an empty teacup.

'Well,' said Fanny. 'We are the old folk of the household now, Aunt Jane, aren't we?'

Over on her side, in the half-light of the flames, her aunt gave a smug smile.

'You will find, dear Fanny,' she said, 'that one of the pleasures of getting older is that one is left in peace on the sofa by the fire and can drink as much wine as one likes. But, Fanny, seriously, why not go? Why not go and just enjoy the dancing? You should, you know. It's been long enough since poor Elizabeth's death.'

'I don't want to go looking for a husband,' Fanny explained.

'But balls aren't *just* about that,' Aunt Jane said. 'There's also the fun of dancing.'

'Oh, not for the younger ladies,' Fanny insisted. 'Underneath, they're all about finding husbands. Don't you remember that you yourself taught me that?'

Aunt Jane laughed.

'I deserved that,' she said. 'I'm old enough to dance at balls just for the fun of it, but maybe not you, not yet. Now listen, Fanny, here's something I've been waiting for a quiet moment to show you. It's a letter from Mr Sprack the thief-taker. I'm not sure that your father would like this, but he's written to ask if you will ever be in London. He says again that he needs an assistant, he says, someone "ladylike", which is how he describes you. Oh, how poor Elizabeth would have been displeased!'

Fanny was so surprised that she could almost have taken it for one of her aunt's jokes.

'Mr Sprack asked after me? Me?'

'Yes,' Aunt Jane insisted. 'He says here –' in the

half-darkness there was a scuffle of the unfolding paper – 'that you were cool as a cucumber. "A regular ice-cold maiden" were his very words. A cool head, he says, is vital in the thief-taking business.'

Fanny remembered the satisfaction of the moment when the trap had been sprung at the temple, and when the thief had been taken. It had almost compensated for the sick terror of the waiting, and the trial of having everyone staring at her while she gave evidence in court.

'What about it, Fanny? I'm going to London next week – perhaps you'll come with me and meet Mr Sprack again?'

'Let me think it over, Aunt Jane,' Fanny said.

How extraordinary, Fanny thought. This was something she could never have imagined a year ago. An invitation to go up to London! An invitation to do something in the world!

Aunt Jane subsided into silence as her book once again consumed her. She tilted it towards the fire and peered at it intently, totally absorbed.

It *was* strangely quiet, Fanny realised. With the children upstairs, the snow outside the windows gave a peaceful feeling. Soon it would be time to draw the curtains, but for now she'd keep them open and watch the snow fall, hoping that it wouldn't fall too fast for the carriage to bring Lizzie home again after the ball.

Fanny remembered how, a year ago, her feelings would have been on fire about the ball. Her whole mind would have been occupied with who she'd dance with, what she'd say to her partners, whether people would think her hair too limp.

'I must put the children to bed,' she said, trying to push out of her mind the thought of the exciting alternative life Mr Sprack wanted her to take.

'Oh no,' said Aunt Jane, standing up at once. 'I'll do it. You deserve a night off.' Without another word she was gone, in one of her sudden and mysterious disappearances.

Fanny sighed, and walked about the library for a second or two, looking for a book to read herself.

Her aunt was right. It was lovely to be quiet, and alone for a while, and not to have to think about either balls or household bills.

What would she like to read?

Her eye travelled over the shelves. All her favourite heroines were here … Eleanor, and Caroline, and Mrs Carrington, who had travelled all the way to Turkey.

Anna is a heroine too, in a quieter way, Fanny thought to herself. *She won't be dancing either tonight.*

She imagined Anna, sitting by the fire at Steventon, placed between her father and her stepmother, mutinous as a mule, perhaps sewing something very badly, plotting, plotting how to escape from her life and weighing up all her options.

Anna would certainly have loved to become a thief-taker's assistant if she'd had the chance. She wouldn't have hesitated for an instant.

Fanny found herself sitting down at her father's desk, and taking her father's pen, and picking it up, playing with it. She was playing, too, with the picture in her mind, of Anna's cross face, her beautiful hair, the passionate way she always spoke, even if she was saying the silliest, lightest thing in the world.

A heroine.

Fanny foraged for a fine, fresh piece of paper, and picked up the pen.

'Anna,' she wrote at the top, like the title of a story.

She underlined it.

She felt like she was poised on the brink of something, like that moment before pushing off on skates for the first time in the winter when the pond froze.

And underneath the title she wrote, 'Miss Austen, Thief-Taker. A Novel of Adventure.'

And then she began.

'Miss Anna Austen, sixteen years of age, was assistant to the celebrated thief-taker, Mr ...'

Yes, if she wasn't going to go out, then at least Fanny would have a thief-taking adventure here at home, and Anna would be the heroine. It would be very pleasant to have a secret.

Epilogue

What happened in real life

Nearly all the characters in this story are real people, from Edward and Elizabeth Austen and their eleven children, to Fanny and Anna themselves, their aunt Jane, and even to Mrs Sackree the children's nurse. Godmersham Park is a real house, still standing in Kent, although Anna's home at Steventon Rectory in Hampshire has since been pulled down.

Aunt Jane often used to stay at her rich brother Edward's house at Godmersham Park, and used her experience of living there to help her imagine some of the big houses she made up and described in the six novels that she wrote in real life. Her family at Godmersham, their servants, their private feuds and their marriages, were vitally important to Aunt Jane and her stories. If you ever find yourself in possession of a ten-pound note, take a close look at it, and you'll find pictures upon it of both Aunt Jane and the mansion of Godmersham Park itself.

The trick played upon Mr Drummer was a real scam which was practised in Georgian England by unscrupulous shopkeepers. In real life, it happened to Aunt Jane's own Aunt Jane, her mother's brother's wife. The lady was accused of stealing a piece of lace from a shop in Bath, and was sent to prison before finally, after a good deal of stressful arguing, being released. The laws in Georgian Britain were designed to protect property, rather than human beings, so it was perfectly possible that you *could* be sent to Australia for something that sounds as trivial as stealing a piece of lace. And if you were a pauper unjustly accused of a crime, it was equally possible that no one would investigate your case fairly, or stand up for you, or help you.

There weren't yet any proper police detectives, and it was the job of every citizen to help solve a crime. The unpaid magistrates who were supposed to administer the system did not always do their work properly, although it has to be said that in real life Edward Austen seems to have been diligent and well respected.

Some people became specialist thief-takers, like

Mr Sprack (a character I've invented). It was a job that was almost like being a private detective today. But the system wasn't always fair. Aunt Jane was quite right to say that before the invention of the police and some reforms to the law in the nineteenth century, justice could often be bought and sold.

In real life, Anna Austen did truly get engaged to one clergyman, Mr Michael Terry, in the teeth of opposition from her parents, only then to throw him over for another, Mr Benjamin Lefroy.

Fanny did eventually change her mind and get married too, at the age of twenty-seven. This was pretty old for a well-off Georgian lady like she was.

If you go to the Hampshire Archives in Winchester, you can read Fanny's real-life diary, all about her brothers and sisters and the death of her mother. There are a lot of exclamation marks in it.

When Fanny's grandmother died, her father, Edward, inherited another big house as well, in addition to Godmersham Park. This one was in Hampshire, and he gave Aunt Jane and her sister, Cassandra, a cottage in which to live in the village nearby, and this is a place that you can still go to visit today because it's run as Jane Austen's House Museum.

Fanny went to live in her father's Hampshire house, would visit Aunt Jane in her cottage nearby every day, read all her novels and loved her dearly.

But Fanny's aunt Jane Austen died at the age of just forty-one.

Fanny herself never wrote a published novel.

Or at least, that's the case as far as we know.

Perhaps, like her aunt, Fanny wrote books secretly, and had their covers simply say that they were 'by a lady'.

Acknowledgements

I first met Fanny and Anna when I was spending a good deal of time with the Austens for the purpose of writing a different book, *Jane Austen at Home*. For my research I visited Fanny's home, Godmersham Park, for which I have to thank Rebecca Lilley, and I learned all about Anna's home, Steventon Rectory, through the generosity of Debbie Charlton. In publishing, I love working with my friends at Bloomsbury, especially Zöe Griffiths and Emily Marples, and I'm thrilled that this is the fourth book I've had illustrated by the marvellous Joe Berger.

Have you read this exciting historical drama
from Lucy Worsley?

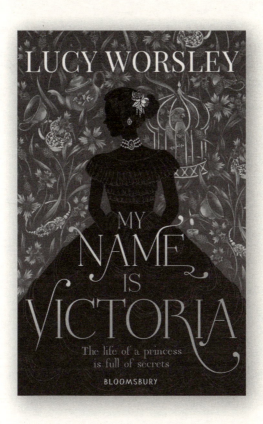

Miss V. Conroy is quiet as a mouse,
and good at keeping secrets. But when she becomes
Princess Victoria's companion, she finds she can
no longer stay in the shadows.

PART ONE

AT
KENSINGTON PALACE

Chapter 1

Journey to the Palace

'Goodbye, Miss V.'

I struggled to reopen the carriage door, for Edward had already clicked it shut before I had had the chance to say farewell properly to my mother. But I was too late. Her stooped back was already disappearing towards the entrance of our house, Arborfield Hall. She had one hand raised to her spine, as usual, as if she found it a great effort to walk.

I gazed after her as she went, giving up my struggle with the handle.

'Have fun!' said Jane, my sister, who did at least manage to reopen the door. She climbed up the step to smack a kiss on to my cheek. 'Goodbye, Dash!' she said, kissing him too and almost smothering him under her ringlets. 'Come back soon with lots of stories.' She jumped back down on to the gravel. 'Maybe you'll have exciting adventures that you can write down into a book of your own,' she added as an afterthought.

'Goodbye, Jane,' I said, although I don't think she heard me. Exciting adventures were the last thing I required. Of course she meant well, but Jane never understood what I might or might not want to do.

I thought she had gone, but here she was bouncing up once more upon the carriage's step. 'Mother *will* miss you, you know, Miss V!' she said. And then, this time, she really did disappear, darting back across the gravel to the house.

I am called 'Miss V. Conroy' because Jane, as the elder, is 'Miss Conroy'.

I am always 'Miss V' so that people will know that I'm not the first Miss Conroy. I was disappointed when my mother told me I would have to carry my 'V' with me, like a limp or an affliction of the speech. I thought I should like to slip through life as 'Miss Conroy'; it sounds more discreet, less noticeable. People always wonder what the 'V' stands for, and they try to find out … I hate that. I hate people knowing about me.

I am good at keeping secrets. I like to be neat and

discreet. I like to sit quiet as a mouse, escaping notice. Hopefully escaping criticism. And that's how I felt that morning when my father jumped into the carriage beside me, and with a jerk of the vehicle we moved off to begin the whole day's journey to London.

Of course my family might use my Christian name; that would be perfectly correct. But my father says that even when I was only one week old, my nursemaids reported that I was already a well-behaved young lady, a 'miss', not a normal, noisy, messy baby.

As our carriage rolled out between the gateposts, it occurred to me that perhaps at our destination for the first time people would call me 'Miss V. Conroy' seriously, and not as a joke. I decided I must prepare myself for the possibility.

I'd been up to London before, of course, with my father, in his blue-painted carriage. But we visited the shops and once the theatre, never staying more than one night. Certainly we had never stayed for several days, as was now the plan. I had packed very carefully, as always, and it had been hard to create space in my trunk for the great number of novels I thought I might need. I was a little anxious that the straps might tug loose and that my trunk and hatbox might fall off the back of our carriage. I kept trying to glimpse them out of the window. Dash was worried too, I could tell, as he sat between my ankles. I rubbed his ears to reassure him.

'Don't worry,' my father said. 'Edward will keep the luggage quite safe.' My father had always had an uncanny ability to read the minds of other people. 'And you will be kept quite safe too, you know,' he added.

I tried to raise a little smile to show that I believed him. I thought, as I often did, of my mother's injunction that I should smile more.

But to be truthful, I didn't quite believe in the new Edward. He was a recent replacement for the old Edward, who had been my friend. All our footmen abandoned their own names and became 'Edward' when they entered my father's service at Arborfield Hall, but they never seemed to stay all that long. I was glad when the last-Edward-but-one had left, for he had been a lazy telltale. The new Edward was so new that I couldn't yet tell if we would be friends. I hoped so.

The thought made me sigh. I wished I had more friends, lots of friends, like my sister Jane. But in truth there was only Dash. It was kind of my father to allow Dash to come with us when it would have been more convenient to have left him behind.

'Now then, Miss V,' my father said, resting his hands on the round brass knob that topped the cane standing between his knees on the carriage floor. He was leaning forward so that his chin almost sat upon his knuckles. As usual, his eyes were twinkling, amused. 'I think,' he said, 'that you and I must have a little confidential conversation before we arrive. I want things to go quite pleasantly, you know.'

I lowered my eyes to my own hands on my lap. 'Pleasantly' was far more than I hoped for from this visit. I wished merely not to disgrace or draw attention to myself.

'You must be excited to be taken to stay at a palace,' he went on. 'And it'll be easy. All you have to do is to play with another little girl. All the girls in London would be glad to take your place! Eh, Miss V?'

In truth I found the prospect as much terrifying as thrilling. This wasn't just any little girl! How would we 'play' together? Could she even play the piano? Would she expect me to entertain her with witty conversation? That would be awful, for I had none.

I glanced up doubtfully.

My father caught this and gave me one of his sharp little nods of encouragement. 'Come on! You can count on me!' he said. 'You can always count on a Conroy,' he added, with a tap of his cane on the floor, 'which means I know that I, in turn, can count on *you*.'

Of course, he was right. Of course I was a lucky girl, and I was fortunate to have a father like him to help me. I'd get through it somehow. With Dash's help too. He was a great icebreaker. Again I stroked his silky brown ears.

My father sat back on the padded seat, quite at ease. There was a pink carnation in his waistcoat. He was watching me with his usual quizzical look. My mother, Lady Elizabeth Conroy, didn't notice much because she was always so tired. But my father noticed everything.

'I know that you're a shy miss,' he said, cocking his head to the side, 'but so is the Other Party.'

'You mean –'

He nodded sharply and flashed his eyes towards the box where Edward sat next to the coachman. Of course. *Not in front of the servants.* I'd been brought up hearing these words every mealtime, every time the conversation got interesting.

'The Other Party …' I hesitated. 'May I ask, please, Papa, how I should address her when we meet?'

'Certainly!' he said. But then a furrow wrinkled his pink forehead. 'I thought your mother would have told you that.'

He leaned forward on his cane and beckoned me nearer to him.

'She is, of course, a princess,' he said very quietly. 'And

you must say, "Your Royal Highness". Never say "Princess", that's not correct when you're talking to her, always "Your Royal Highness". And wait until she speaks to you. And you know your curtsey?'

I bent my chin again, right down to my chest. My mother *had* said something vague to me about curtseys earlier this morning, but it had been in her usual dreamy manner. She had not been well recently. In fact, I could not remember her being perfectly well in my whole life.

For a second, I had to blink hard to clear my eyes. This had been one of our mother's bad mornings, when she had gone straight from her bed to recline on the chaise longue in the window, hardly stopping to dress herself properly on the way. On days like these she seemed reconciled to staying put there in her nightgown until dinnertime.

'Of course you know your curtsey, don't you, Miss V?' she'd murmured, not turning her head, as I'd crept across the carpet towards her to remind her of our departure. Well, I thought I knew my curtsey, but I wasn't entirely sure. And I hadn't dared to ask her for clarification.

Now I reminded myself fiercely that it had been a great step for her to have come down from her bedroom to see us off at all.

'I … think I know how to curtsey, Papa.'

It was the wrong thing to say. His eyebrows shot

forward and his hands tightened on that brass knob as if he wanted to hurt it. 'My God!' he said. 'My dearly beloved family have cotton wool for brains. Sometimes I think the good Lord has sent them specifically to try my patience.' He fell to looking crossly out of the window, and silence reigned.

I waited, mute, a careful hand on Dash's head to warn him that now was no time to wriggle or bark.

Eventually my father's eyes wandered back inside the carriage and I tensed myself to take the pressure of his gaze. Surely he would not be cross today, with all the excitement and strangeness of departure. I was sitting demurely on the seat, knees squeezed together, my hair smoothly looped up at each side of my head – not falling forward in torrents of ringlets like the fashionable girls wore – waiting anxiously for the storm to pass.

I was right. He was smiling again.

'Well, Miss V,' he said. My father's temper tantrums never lasted long. 'You certainly have more common sense than the rest of them.' By this he meant not only my mother and Jane but also my three boisterous brothers.

'You at least are quiet and obedient,' he said. 'And I know,' he added a little more kindly, 'that you'll miss that wretched little hound of yours. What's his name, again? Is it Splash?'

'Dash! It's Dash!'

Upon hearing his name, Dash sat up straight and raised his tiny chin as if to look my father in the eye. Dash! He was such a good dog, so well trained, so quiet and clean. He really was a comfort to me as we went about our daily business at Arborfield Hall: the shrubbery walk, piano practice, needlework. When I was sitting behind the curtain in the library with a volume of Sir Walter's in my lap, it was Dash who would first hear and warn me of the tread of the housemaid with the coal scuttle, giving me time to hop up neatly and put the forbidden book back. It was Dash who kissed me before I went to sleep at night.

But what did my father mean about my 'missing' Dash? Surely he wasn't going to be sent back to Arborfield Hall? Before I could ask, he spoke again.

'Well, young Dash!' My father prodded Dash with his cane. 'How are you going to enjoy being a royal dog? That's a distinguished canine band to be joining, and no mistake!'

I was speechless. What could he mean? I felt the shameful crimson rising up my neck, as it so often did.

'Oh, *Lord*!' he said as he saw me blush. 'Confound it! Can it be that my dear wife has failed to explain?'

He knocked his cane once or twice on the floor in his

exasperation. His eyes always seemed to flash theatrically, like those of the enchanter we had seen in last year's pantomime. 'Miss V, my apologies, but I thought you knew. The dog is to be your gift to the Other Party, of course.'

'But ...'

My breath failed me. Give away my dog? To this unknown girl? I gripped my hands tighter together. Dash could sense that something was wrong. He knew his own name, the dear, dear hound.

'It's just a senseless brute, Miss V,' he said, with vexation. 'And it's of the utmost importance that you make a friend of this ... erm, this child you're going to meet today,' he went on.

Despite my efforts, I felt a fat tear welling up in my eye. I tried to pretend it wasn't there. I felt utterly incapable of reaching for my handkerchief.

'Oh, come, come, my dear!' he said, pulling out his own handkerchief and shoving it roughly into my hand.

'Perhaps I have miscalculated,' he said quietly, as if to himself, and once again his gaze seemed drawn away from me, out of the window. I felt sore inside. I loved Dash desperately, but then I loved my father even more.

'I thought that you would be a good girl, Miss V,' he said. 'Equal to this task. You can do it, eh? You can give up your dog in order to make a fine first impression? The party has asked me specifically for a dog, exactly like this one! Come, come, don't let me down. Otherwise I'll have to send you back to the country and find myself a new Miss V from somewhere else.' He gestured vaguely out of the window, as if daughters were to be picked up anywhere. 'And I'm sure I won't like the new one half as much.'

Now his attention was trained back upon me, like a beam of light concentrated by a prism glass. As always, when he *really* looked at me, I felt the warmth of his gaze.

'You're a brave little miss, aren't you?' he said cajolingly. 'And you know that it's your duty to win this little girl over, don't you? To make friends with her?'

Reluctantly, I sniffed and nodded.

'My post depends on you, Miss V!'

My father was the comptroller to the Duchess of Kent, the princess's mother. He often spoke proudly of his position in a royal household, and the advantages and connections it brought to us.

'You know that the Duchess of Kent is our patroness? And that's why we can live at Arborfield Hall and drive in a carriage, and why in a day or two, when I have a moment and when one or two bills have been dealt with, I'll be able to buy you another little puppy to replace that one.'

The thought of another puppy was horrible.

'But I love Dash,' I coughed. 'And he loves me!'

'You'll have another puppy, my dear, but the first chance to impress the princess will never come again,' he said. 'I regret it, but it really is for the best that you give her your dog.'

At that he folded his arms, throwing himself back on his seat and returning his gaze to the passing fields and damp meadows.

And so, as we sat in miserable silence, all thoughts of home wiped from my mind by this catastrophe, my hand crept down again to rest on Dash's head. I tried not to think of his life with another girl. I tried to not think of the wet, whiskery kisses he gave me, nor of his cushion, his bowl or his little felt toy mouse that I had last night packed lovingly into the corner of my trunk.

How could I endure our stay in this horrible place where Dash, my only friend, was to be taken from me? How could I possibly return to Arborfield Hall without him? And how on earth could I make friends with his thief?

Look out for more exciting historical drama from Lucy Worsley

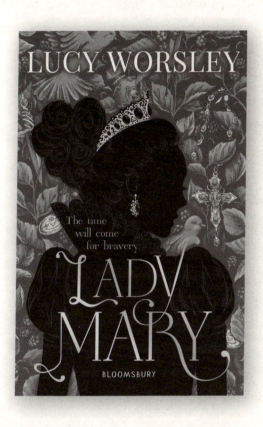

Mary Tudor's world is turned upside down when her father, Henry the Eighth, declares that his marriage to her mother is over and Mary isn't really his child. Banished from court and alone for the first time in her life, Mary must fight for what is rightfully hers.

Look out for more exciting historical drama
from Lucy Worsley

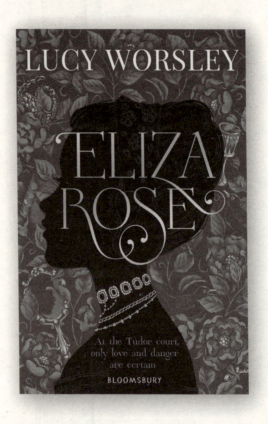

Eliza Camperdowne is young and headstrong,
but she knows her duty. She must one day marry
a man who is very grand and very rich. But fate has
other plans. When she becomes a maid of honour,
she's drawn into the thrilling, treacherous
court of Henry the Eighth …